"I thought you weren't coming home until late," Liss said, surprised.

"I changed my mind," Kirk said. "This is my home, too, and I won't be forced out of it."

"I wasn't aware of having forced you out," she said.

"You didn't," he said. Abruptly, he reached out and caught her around the waist, his cold hands startling on her bare skin where her shirt had hitched up. "This did."

"What—" she started to say, but something in his expression silenced her. His eyes glittered under the brim of his hat. His chest rose and fell within the open front of his jacket. His powerful thighs brushed against hers, and his long fingers flexed on her waist. He bent low, held her tight against him, and kissed her for a long moment.

"I kept thinking how you tasted this morning, how you felt in my arms. I wondered if it would still be the same." He stroked his fingers along her cheek. "My memory didn't lie, but this time was better." He grinned. "Now you taste like chocolate cake, and I love chocolate. . . ."

WHAT ARE *LOVESWEPT* ROMANCES?

They are stories of true romance and touching emotion. We believe those two very important ingredients are constants in our highly sensual and very believable stories in the *LOVESWEPT* line. Our goal is to give you, the reader, stories of consistently high quality that may sometimes make you laugh, sometimes make you cry, but are always fresh and creative and contain many delightful surprises within their pages.

Most romance fans read an enormous number of books. Those they truly love, they keep. Others may be traded with friends and soon forgotten. We hope that each *LOVESWEPT* romance will be a treasure—a "keeper." We will always try to publish

LOVE STORIES YOU'LL NEVER FORGET
BY AUTHORS YOU'LL ALWAYS REMEMBER

The Editors

Judy Gill
Dangerous Proposition

BANTAM BOOKS
NEW YORK · TORONTO · LONDON · SYDNEY · AUCKLAND

DANGEROUS PROPOSITION

A Bantam Book / November 1991

*If you would be interested in receiving protective vinyl
covers for your Loveswept books, please write to this address
for information:*

*Loveswept
Bantam Books
P.O. Box 985
Hicksville, NY 11802*

ISBN 0-553-44195-7

Published simultaneously in the United States and Canada

*Bantam Books are published by Bantam Books, a division
of Bantam Doubleday Dell Publishing Group, Inc. Its trademark, consisting of the words "Bantam Books" and the
portrayal of a rooster, is Registered in U.S. Patent and
Trademark Office and in other countries. Marca Registrada.
Bantam Books, 666 Fifth Avenue, New York, New York
10103.*

PRINTED IN THE UNITED STATES OF AMERICA

OPM   0 9 8 7 6 5 4 3 2 1

For my brother and sister-in-law,
David and Sharon Griffith,
for their kids,
their cows,
their mountains,
but most of all, heaven help them,
for their snow!

One

Ryan McCall woke up from his nap, stared out the car window, and shouted, "Look, Mom! Snow!"

Liss Tremayne glanced at her excited four-year-old in the rearview mirror. "Hush. I know. Don't wake Jason."

"Snowing," she thought, inaccurately described the blizzard that had been raging for the past forty-five minutes. In the last fifteen minutes, all the road markings had been obliterated, and her four-wheel-drive Blazer kept threatening to forge a trail of its own, straight into the ditch. She'd gone from extremely nervous to downright terrified but was determined not to let Ryan see. She ground her molars together and fought the wheel, slowing as a huge gust of wind slammed into the side of the Blazer, carrying a load of snow that obscured her vision for several seconds.

Lord, what had she gotten herself into? Liss wondered, putting another soothing tape into the cassette player as soon as she could take one hand off the wheel for a second. Was she, as her in-laws insisted, out of her mind for leaving the safe, familiar city where she'd always lived and, on the last day of November, taking her children off into the wilderness? More precisely, to a cattle ranch, where they weren't wanted and where they would have to share a house with a man she didn't know and an old lady with a grudge against the world. Maybe she was out of her mind, but even if she and her sons weren't wanted, her late uncle Ambrose Whittier's will had offered a chance for her to make a better home for her children than she'd managed to in Vancouver.

There were going to be problems, though, and far worse ones than snow. Kirk Allbright had seemed so nice when he'd picked her up at her house that morning at the beginning of the month. His slow smile had done crazy things to her insides, and when he'd shoved his silver-gray Stetson to the back of his head, letting a thick swath of straight dark-blond hair fall over his forehead, she'd gone weak in the knees. Half an hour later, the two of them had tacitly allied themselves against Mrs. Healey, Uncle Ambrose's forbidding, elderly former housekeeper. She had done nothing but carp and complain from the moment they arrived at her house until the lawyer finally shut her up by saying that she, along with Liss and Kirk, had inherited a one-third share in Whittier Ranch. But, he'd added, they each had to agree to live there if they wanted to inherit.

That was when Liss had learned that Kirk Allbright was Uncle Ambrose's illegitimate son, and that he'd expected to inherit alone. His smiling gray eyes had gone cold and hard, and his mouth had formed a straight, taut line as he glared at her, silently accusing her of having somehow arranged all of this.

Liss clenched her teeth and wrapped her hands

tightly around the wheel. She fought another skid before she remembered to relax her grip and steer in the skid's direction. Carefully, cautiously, she brought the car back under control. *What a road!* she thought. *What a night!* If only she hadn't stopped all those times along the beautiful Coquihalla Highway to take rolls and rolls of photographs. But the sky had been blue and cloudless then. The mountains and the endless vistas, roaring streams and cascading waterfalls, had cried out to be captured. She'd been unable to resist the vision of merchandising and advertising executives gasping in awe at her expertise, her knowledge of form and composition, her sheer artistry. She had stopped in the town of Merritt to send the films to what had once been her favorite lab, with instructions for them to forward the finished products on to Graham James, her agent.

Now, though, she thought she might pay dearly for the delay, instead of having the photos pay her the dazzling sums she'd fantasized.

"Can we make a snowman when we get there?" Ryan asked in a lower voice.

Liss peered through the swirling white and again fought the car's tendency to slide out of control. "It'll be too late and too cold then, honey," she said, and shivered. Suddenly she was more glad than ever that the lawyer, Lester Brown, had helped her choose this four-wheel-drive vehicle and had advanced her the funds from her first quarter's dividend to buy warm winter clothing for herself and the kids.

"We could build it under the street lamp like we did last year," Ryan said hopefully.

Liss smiled. They'd done that because the weatherman had predicted rain by morning. "There'll be lots of time to build snowmen at the ranch," she said. "This snow won't melt overnight, I promise you."

Street lamp? she thought. Hah! She hadn't seen a street lamp for fifty miles, or a town, or a lighted house, or another car. She wondered if she'd see green grass before June, and swallowed hard. Since news of her move had gotten out, everyone she knew had some horror story to tell her—about the nine- and ten-foot snowfalls in the Robson Valley, close up against the sheer western slopes of the Rockies; about temperatures of forty below zero; about what happened to people who got caught outside under such conditions.

But going to Whittier Ranch or not going there might become a moot point if she couldn't keep the damned car on the road, she told herself, and concentrated harder on her driving. She had chosen to ignore those horror stories and shrug off all the "good" advice she'd been offered. She and her children had a right to their place on the ranch, and she wouldn't be stopped, not by the weather, not by Mrs. Healey's bad manners, not even by Kirk Allbright's attitude. There was nothing anybody could do to keep her out.

The dog was huge. It stood between Liss and the front door of the house, its hackles up, its snarling mouth open to reveal sharp teeth. Snow swirled around it, doing nothing to cool its rage at the intrusion of her car into the smooth, unplowed driveway that led to the front of the house.

She had tried to open the car door, but the dog had barked ferociously and lunged toward her the instant the dome light came on. She'd slammed the door and, inanely, locked it.

"What are we going to do?" Ryan asked.

"Sit here and blow the horn until Mr. Allbright comes out to call off his hound." She gave the horn another blast.

"Maybe he's not home," Jason said. He and his brother leaned forward and hooked their elbows over the back of her seat. Their combined breath was warm on her neck as they, too, watched the furious dog.

Liss herself had been wondering where Kirk Allbright was. She'd been blowing the horn for ten minutes with no luck. This was Friday evening. He might not be home for hours. He might not come home at all, she realized. He likely had a hot date on this cold night. What if he was away for the weekend? For two cents, she'd turn around and head home—except that conditions were so bad she knew she wouldn't make it, and she didn't think freezing to death in a ditch beside an empty, endless highway would be any better than freezing to death here. Besides, *this* was home for her and the kids now.

She sighed. Fat lot of good it did to sit there telling herself she had a right to get into that house, when between her and the front door was a dog about as vicious as the highway behind her. *But wait*, she thought. *"Front door" suggested "back door."* Liss smiled grimly. Right. She was not going to sit here and watch her children freeze! She shifted into drive and crept slowly around the house, peering at the place for any sign of occupancy. There was none, until she saw the dim yellow glow of a porch light. Relief washed through her.

The door under that light was mercifully unlocked, and it led into an entryway that obviously served as a pantry and laundry room. It was nearly as large as her entire former house had been, and yet was only half the size of the kitchen beyond it.

It took ten minutes to get everything out of the Blazer and into the house, and by the time she was finished, Liss was wet, exhausted, and half frozen. She staggered into the kitchen and dropped the last suitcase on the floor, then carefully dusted snow off her largest camera case and set it beside the other one on the end of the table. Those cameras were important, and becoming more important as each moment passed, she decided, looking around in dull disgust at the dirt and clutter. Something sticky and brown had oozed down the side of the stove and pooled onto the floor. Jason knelt in it as he and Ryan bent over a box beside the stove.

"Look, Mom!" Ryan's brown eyes gleamed under his straight bangs. "Kitties. A big mama cat and little bitty babies."

She smiled and slumped against the fridge. They were there, safe, and together, and that was all that mattered. As Ryan picked up a kitten to show her, mama cat reared up with a hiss and swiped at his face, her claws bared. Startled, he dropped the kitten into its soft nest and leaped back while Liss jumped forward to haul Jason out of the cat's reach. Ryan's eyes flooded as he wailed, "The kitty scratched me!" Not to be outdone, Jason cried, too.

Crouching, Liss gathered both boys close, soothing them and then cheering them with the promise of food. She managed an adequate meal for them of scrambled eggs and toast. While they ate, she explored, munching a slice of toast and finding the rest of the house in the same state of chaos as the kitchen. There were plenty of bedrooms on the second floor. One was obviously Kirk's, and another, at the end of the far wing, was also occupied—by a soundly sleeping, loudly snoring, completely oblivious Mrs. Healey, who apparently didn't object to living in squalor. With a shudder at the sight of the littered room, Liss closed the door and returned to the one she'd chosen for the boys, to make up their beds.

When the children had finished eating, she carried Jason and led a worn-out Ryan by the hand to their new room, telling them she'd be sleeping right next door. They were asleep almost before she finished pulling up their covers, and she headed back downstairs for the rest of their things.

Leaning on the kitchen table, she looked at the opened suitcases spread over the floor, their contents jumbled from the boys' search for pajamas. Exhaustion washed over her as she thought about carrying those bags upstairs. No. She couldn't do it. She was too tired. She'd scramble some of those eggs for herself and then go to bed. The mess could wait till tomorrow. Who'd notice her clutter amid that which already existed?

With her eggs cooking, she lifted one of her suitcases to the table and sought a nightgown and robe. She had just found the former when the back door opened on a gust of cold wind and two snowy figures stumbled inside and staggered kitchen-ward.

Liss didn't even think. She simply recognized the first of those figures as a deadly enemy and reacted, sweeping up the entire suitcase and flinging it at the intruders with a scream of pure terror.

"Back! Back!" she cried frantically. "Sit! Lie down! Outside! Go home!" She snatched up a chair and held it threateningly before her as she edged around the table, putting more and more obstacles between herself and the snow-covered animal that ambled into the kitchen, looking stunned and slightly abashed with a lacy pink bra hanging out of his mouth and a pair of panties over his high, curving tail.

Kirk Allbright gaped at the woman who had invaded his kitchen with several suitcases and boxes, then slowly peeled off his thick leather gloves and unbuttoned his sheepskin jacket. Bending, he lifted the panties from their perch on his dog's bushy tail and dangled them from one finger. Liss Tremayne, her face as white as the underwear he held, still held a chair in front of her as if she would fling it as she had the suitcase. She backed around the table as she shouted conflicting orders at his perfectly harmless and undoubtedly confused dog.

She was dressed in jeans and a thick red sweater. Her nearly black hair tumbled loose around her shoulders, and her almond-shaped eyes were huge with terror, pinned on the dog. When she came up against the counter, she stopped of necessity and stared at Kirk as if only then becoming aware of his presence.

"Call him off," she begged, her voice shaking. "Please send him away. Oh, Lord, he's eating my bra!"

Kirk took the bra from Marsh's slack jaws and dangled it from the same finger as the panties. "Sit, Marsh." Obediently, the dog, a cross between a husky and a shepherd, lowered himself onto his haunches, tongue lolling, ears pricked up, head cocked. "Stay," Kirk added, and bent to pick up the spilled suitcase, stuffing items of feminine apparel back in it willy-nilly. He set it on the table, put his snow-damp Stetson on top of the fridge, then walked over to her, taking the chair from her and setting it on the floor.

"Hello, Liss," he said, and groaned silently. At close quarters, her scent affected him exactly as it had the day he'd met her. He told himself it shouldn't, that he couldn't let it. In spite of himself, he drew in a deep breath of it and extended his hand.

His words seemed to whip her into action. She slapped his hand aside and glared at him. "'Hello'?" she shouted. "'Hello'? Is that all you can say after leaving a vicious animal chained between the driveway and the door when you're expecting someone to arrive? What kind of monster are you, not to be here when that person and her two innocent little children show up in the middle of a blizzard, and can't get inside the house because there's nobody around to call off the animal? And now you come waltzing in here after a nice, cozy evening out with one of your women while I've been out there on your stupid treacherous country roads, driving through the dark and the snow without another car in sight for miles and miles, and not even a motel or a town or anything, and then coming in and finding this pigsty waiting for me and you have the gall to say '*hello*'?" She gasped for breath and flung an arm in a wide sweep around the kitchen. Kirk winced.

It was a pigsty. He had to admit it. But it had been one hell of a week, and he hadn't had time to do much more than work and catch an hour or two of sleep before going back out to work some more. It was that or lose cattle, and now that the ranch had to support three adults and two children, he couldn't afford to take any chances.

Before he could begin to explain, Liss carried on, her voice growing more shrill. "Did you figure you could leave this mess for weeks and weeks simply because I was coming to clean it all up? I didn't come to be a servant to you, Kirk Allbright! I didn't come to have my children threatened by a man-eating beast! Even your damned cat clawed at Ryan and . . . and . . . I must have been out of my mind to think this would be a safe place to raise my children, but don't think your snow or your mean animals or your mess is going to drive me away! Move!" she added, pushing him hard as her voice cracked and tears spurted from her dark eyes. "Get out of my way! I'm going to bed!"

Her tears undid his tight control. Dammit, he was tired, and hungry, and cold, and he didn't need a woman screaming at him the minute he got home from a long and exhausting day. He'd been racing the weather for the past three days, and every one of them had been hell. And now this! The nerve of her, berating him about going out with women, as if it were any of her affair what he did. This was exactly what he'd been afraid of when he'd learned he was to have her and the old bat dumped on him! Mrs. Healey's behavior since her arrival the previous week had been enough to deal with, and now here came this one, pulling that one female trick geared to turn a man inside out. Well, he'd had enough of women this past week. Hell, the past year!

He blocked her way. "Now, you just wait one damn minute here, lady. How the hell was I supposed to know you were coming today when you didn't tell me? I'm not a mind reader!"

She dashed the tears from her eyes. "I wrote to tell you I was coming today."

"Yeah? When?"

Liss had to think about it. The past weeks had been a whirl of activity, of getting packed, of saying good-bye to friends, of one last, horrendous battle with Johnny's folks. She felt tears well up again and held them back with a conscious effort of will. "On—on Monday, I think." Or had it been Tuesday before the letter got mailed?

Kirk stared at her. Her chin trembled! It honest-to-goodness trembled. How many hours had she spent practicing in front of a mirror to learn how to do that?

"Oh, for the love of Mike!" he roared. "Where the hell do you think you are, city girl? Letters don't arrive in an hour or two out here! A letter mailed in the city on Monday won't show up here before Friday at the earliest, and Tuesday was the last day I had time to drive into town to pick up mail. What do you think I'm running here, a nine-to-five operation? I've been beating myself into the ground trying to get feed out to my cows before this storm hit. And why the hell were you driving in these conditions anyway? You should have holed up in a motel at the first warning!"

Hands on her hips, she yelled right back at him, "What warning?"

"On the radio, of course. Doesn't that fancy Blazer you and Lester Brown picked out have a radio in it?"

Liss blinked rapidly, stung by the acidity of his tone. "Are you objecting to the car we chose? Lester said *you* specifically stipulated a four-wheel-drive vehicle, so that's what we got. After all, it's not mine any more than it's yours. It belongs to the ranch, so what's your problem?"

"My 'problem,' as you so sweetly put it, is that you risked your and your children's lives by failing to exercise common sense. The weather advisory has been on the air since day before yesterday with frequent updates. What I want to know is why weren't you listening?"

She stared up into his furious gray eyes. And to think she'd once thought he was attractive! To think that during the half-hour drive to the lawyer's office, before any of them knew they were going to live together, he'd made her stomach quiver with nothing more than a smile. Now, as during the reading of the will, he was glaring at her as if everything were her fault. Instead of making her stomach quiver, he was making it churn.

"I was playing my tapes," she said through clenched teeth. "I hadn't heard any of them for ages, and I was enjoying them. Why would I want to listen to some mouthy deejay when I don't have to?"

He rolled his eyes and shook his head in disgust. "Because that mouthy deejay might have told you to get the hell off the road if you didn't have a damned good reason to be there. So, I'm telling you, city girl, from her on you listen to the radio at least once every hour while winter lasts. Failing that, open your eyes and pay attention to the warnings all around you. The minute it started snowing, you should have started looking for a motel."

"Look for a motel because of a few snowflakes? Would you?"

"Damn right I would, if I was driving into unknown territory and unused to the conditions."

"How could I know how bad it was going to get? And it was pretty at first. Then—then all of a sudden the road disappeared." She paused to draw in a deep breath, trying to steady her voice. "And so did all the towns and lights, and all I could do was keep coming until I saw the ranch sign and when I got here there was nothing but that horrible animal out there w-with his teeth bared to keep me away and . . ." She felt a choking sensation in her throat and turned her head away. "And I thought you'd be here." It was hardly more than a whisper.

Kirk nearly groaned aloud. Having her hide her tears was worse than letting him see them. Worse, and sneakier, and far more manipulative. He steeled himself. "I have a ranch to run. I couldn't sit around waiting for you to show up so I could say welcome, especially when you're not."

She looked at him then, and there were no tears, no quivering chin, just a deep, abiding weariness and an ineffable sadness in her face. "I know I'm not," she said. "But I couldn't let that matter, you see. I had to come anyway. For the kids."

Before he could stop her, she slipped around him and snatched up the suitcase she'd thrown at the dog. Tucking it under her arm, she left the room without looking back.

Oh, hell, what had made him say she wasn't welcome? he wondered as he looked through the doorway toward the stairs, listening to her ascend. It was a filthy thing to say to a woman whose only fault was that, because she resembled a long-dead relation she probably didn't even remember, she'd been left part of his ranch. She'd likely had as long and exhausting a day as he'd had, and was as tired as he was, maybe even as hungry.

Hungry? It was then that he smelled scorching food and looked at the stove. A congealed mess that had once been scrambled eggs now smoked in a pan, turning brown around the edges.

With a growl of disgust, Kirk lifted the pan and shoved it, eggs and all, into the overloaded sink, then sat down at the table and pulled off his boots, leaving them lying where they fell. He was too damned tired to do anything else.

Liss lay on her bed, tears slowly leaking from her eyes. She was feeling sorry, not for herself, of course, but for poor Uncle Ambrose, a cold, hard man who'd been embittered by his young bride's death. At least that's what Liss's father had told her, and she figured he should know. His sister had been Ambrose's wife. How sad, Liss thought, that her aunt had died in childbirth, along with the infant, leaving Ambrose with this huge, empty house. Kirk was equally as cold, every bit as hard, as Ambrose was reputed to have been, but what was his excuse?

Greed, she told herself, and pique at not being his natural father's sole heir.

She groaned softly when that not sole heir knocked on her door. "Go away," she said, rubbing hastily at her cheeks with the sleeve of her sweater.

He didn't. The door opened and he stepped in, still wearing the same damp jeans, but minus his boots and jacket. The three-day growth of beard remained. His eyes were dark and tired, and so oddly compassionate that she had to look away lest the kindness undo her completely and start the tears again. She rolled off the bed and walked over to the window, standing with her back to the room.

"Please, go away," she repeated.

Kirk knew he should do as she asked, but something about the stiff set of her slim shoulders, the guarded quality in her posture, held him there. Walking away from her right then would be like turning his back on a child in pain. Stocking feet silent on the carpeted floor, he approached her. When he reached out and touched her shoulder, he felt her flinch, then become so rigid, he thought her muscles might snap.

"Come here," he said quietly, urging her to turn around and face him.

Liss clenched her teeth, trying not to hear the soft tenderness in his tone. She wanted to resist, but his hand on her shoulder was hard and warm as he turned her. She couldn't look up at him, only stared at the red-and-black plaid of his flannel shirt, watching it blur and swim before her. This close, she was suddenly aware that he smelled of leather and sweat and dried grass, a not unpleasant combination, but disturbingly masculine.

"Come on, Liss," he said, his voice quiet and deep. "I'm sorry I said you weren't welcome. Believe me, you're a whole lot more welcome than our third partner in this venture. I was . . . I guess I was responding in kind to the way you greeted me, but I shouldn't have. I know you were badly scared and had a lot of adrenaline to use up, and that's what all the shouting and crying was about. I shouldn't have said what I did and hurt your feelings."

He felt her struggle to move away from him, but he grasped her other shoulder and held her firmly. The wool of her soft red sweater caught on the rough skin of his hands, making him achingly aware of her fragile femininity and his own masculinity. It was not a difference he wanted to be reminded of. All he'd come for was to apologize for saying something he shouldn't have said, something that wasn't true. She wasn't exactly unwelcome. It was just that he'd need time to get used to having someone like her around. A woman. Soft. Delicate. Someone who smelled good. Someone who cried.

He drew in a deep, unsteady breath. "Please, don't cry anymore."

"I'm not crying," she said huskily.

"No?" He ran a finger up one side of her face, collecting tears to show her. Her skin was silky and warm. He hoped his frost-roughened finger hadn't hurt her. Damn, but she was little! And vulnerable, seeming to lack the strength to fight off bullies, among whom he counted himself at the moment. "What's this?" he asked, showing her his finger.

She wiped her eyes with the heels of her hands and shook her head. "All right, so I'm crying. But not because I was scared or because you hurt my feelings. I always cry when I'm mad, and I lost my temper because of the blizzard coming up without warning, and the dirty house and the mean animals and that fat old lady sleeping down the hall with her hearing aids out and not hearing me honk and honk and . . . and . . . Oh, heavens, I was so sca-a-ared, Kirk! So damned scared that . . . my b-babies . . . were going to die in the cold and . . ."

Instinctively his arms went around her, offering solace and protection and— He shuddered at the delicate warmth of her, the soft press of her breasts against his chest, the scent of her dark hair, the silky feel of it under his chin. "Hush," he murmured, "I know, I know. But you got here, Liss, you did it, and your children are warm and safe and the dog wouldn't have hurt you. He's noisy but gentle, and I didn't tie him out there. It wasn't me, I swear that. Everything will be okay. There, now, rest on me."

Liss didn't know why, but with a huge sigh, she leaned on him, burrowing closer and sliding her arms around his waist as he stroked her hair. The heavy, steady beat of his heart drowned out the sound of screaming wind and hard snow pelting the window in an unending stream. Oh, heavens, it felt so good, being held like this, she thought dimly, her head swirling with weariness and sensual reaction.

She was a sweet, warm armful, Kirk thought, feeling his exhaustion fade away as her heat penetrated his clothing. No, only half an armful. Lord, but she was little. His hand skimmed over her cheek, drying her tears, and he felt how small and delicate the bones seemed. He squeezed her shoulder through her thick sweater, then slid one thumb inside the ribbing at its neckline and stroked her skin. He stopped when he encountered a pulse-point, and felt the fluttering throb of her blood. He filled his other hand with her soft, scented hair and tugged gently so she raised her head. She looked up at him with her damp, exotic eyes, and he bent low, his lips brushing hers. Need slammed into him, and without thinking he parted her lips with his tongue. The steady yet slightly accelerated pulse in her throat went wild beneath his thumb. She returned his kiss with incredible sweetness, giving and trusting and coming with him as he backed up to that inviting bed behind him.

Two

Suddenly, Kirk realized what he was doing, and with whom. He jerked erect and set her from him. No damn way! he told himself. He refused to respond to Liss in that way, refused to submit to any kind of from-the-grave matchmaking Brose might have intended. He wasn't stupid. He knew what the old man had been up to and he wasn't buying into it! Throwing a woman on him like this! Setting him up with a soft, feminine person right under his own roof and taking the initiative away from him. *Lotsa luck, Brose!* he said silently. *The ones I want, I bring in myself. And then I send them away when I'm done.*

Liss nearly groaned aloud with shame as Kirk pushed her away from him, away from the warmth she'd snuggled into as if she had a right to be there. He rubbed a hand over his heavy growth of beard, and the rasping sound sent a quiver through her insides. She'd even liked the way those whiskers had felt on her face.

"Sorry," he said gruffly.

She lifted her gaze to his face. His expression

was remote, his eyes hooded. His taut mouth had a pale circle around it, exactly the way it'd had when he'd learned she intended to move to the ranch.

She stepped back, wiping her hand over her mouth as if to erase the feel of him. "I apologize, too," she said stiffly, "for falling apart."

He blinked, looking startled, as if he weren't accustomed to people apologizing to him. He even sounded surprised. "*You* didn't do anything to be sorry for. I—I came to tell you that I've scrambled a bunch more eggs. Would you like some? Yours burned."

More than her scrambled eggs had burned, she thought. Her entire body burned from that one short yet extremely explosive kiss. She wanted to refuse his offer. She wanted to crawl into her bed and sleep for several months. Again, she became aware of the pellets of snow hammering the windows, of the wind whistling in the eaves. She shivered. Bears knew what they were doing, hibernating throughout winter. But in only a few hours, she'd have two active little boys needing her, to say nothing of a house so dirty it would take a team of workers a month to get it back into shape. Only she didn't have a team. She had herself. She'd need her strength, and she wouldn't get it starving herself because she was scared of—of a little bit of snow.

"Thanks," she said, lifting her chin determinedly. "I could do with some food."

Liss eyed the big dog warily. Apart from getting up and gobbling the food Kirk emptied into its bowl, though, it lay in the entry-cum-utility room, its chin on its paws, watching as she and Kirk cleared off the kitchen table and set places for their late supper.

"What's his name?" she asked.

Kirk took a plate of toast from the oven and set it on the table, then poured hot chocolate from the potful Liss had made, slopping some on his thumb. She had to smile as he licked it off exactly as one of her children would have. "Marshal," he said, "Marsh for short. Right from the start, he marshaled his littermates, even his mother, keeping everyone in order. He took on the geese on the ranch where he was born, too. Later, he did it with Brose and me and the hands, even before I trained him to herd cows." Kirk grinned. "Don't be surprised to find him herding your kids. Just remember, he won't harm them."

She sat down, giving the dog another wary look. That remained to be seen, she thought. She wasn't prepared to trust the animal for one millisecond. She had seen those teeth of his bare inches from her ankle, and had never forgotten the one time a dog sank its fangs into her. Well, one fang. She had a scar on her chin to prove it. "If you say so. How many hands—uh, workers—do you have?"

"We," he said pointedly. "Remember, we're in this together now. But at this time of year, I run the ranch alone. In March, when calving starts, we hire a full-time man and keep him on till fall roundup is over, and bring in part-timers as needed."

She paused with a forkful of eggs halfway to her mouth. "Roundup? Really? Like in the movies?"

He grinned at her wide-eyed reaction. "Exactly. Horses, lassos, branding, the works. Do you ride?"

Apprehension swept through her as she pictured herself on horseback, trying to rope a steer.

His grin broadened as he appeared to read her

mind, or maybe simply her face. "You don't like horses?"

She shrugged and ate her eggs. They were deliciously fresh. "It's not so much that I don't like them. But they're awfully big and, well, the only time I was ever aboard one, it put its head down to eat and I slid right off over its nose."

He laughed, a warm and pleasant sound she found herself responding to much too readily. "I'd love to have seen that."

In spite of herself, she laughed with him. "My dad thought it was pretty funny, too, but I didn't. I was sure the horse was going to start chomping on me when I fell into its hay. I got up and ran like the blazes back to where we were camping, so my mother could save me from girl-eating equines. I was six." She fixed a leery gaze on his face. "I won't have to learn to ride, will I?"

He shook his head. "No, not unless you want to, but come spring, when we get ponies for the boys and they're learning, you might change your mind. Remember," he added before she could dispute his assumption that her boys would be learning to ride in the spring, "under the terms of Brose's will, your concern is the house. I won't call on you to do any ranching chores, like roundup or branding."

Ah, yes, she thought. No ranching chores, just the cooking, the cleaning, the kids . . . Clearly, Uncle Ambrose had never come fully up-to-date in the division of labor, although Mrs. Healey, his former housekeeper and, Liss suspected, lover, had been given the task of keeping the books as her contribution to the three-way inheritance. "Who did the housework before?" she asked. "I mean, in the years between Mrs. Healey's leaving and the present time?"

"Brose, mostly." She saw a flicker of emotion cross his face. Of course, she mused. He must miss his father. From what she'd learned in the lawyer's office, Kirk hadn't met Ambrose Whittier until he was thirty. Naturally, in the seven or eight years they'd been together, real affection would have united them. She wished she hadn't asked about the housekeeping and sought a new topic of conversation. Unwillingly, she remembered something else Lester Brown had said when describing her contribution to the ranch, something she'd succeeded in putting out of her mind because she hadn't wanted to think about it until she had to.

All those eggs must mean . . . chickens.

She lifted her gaze to Kirk's face. "Did Ambrose look after the chickens as well?"

Kirk looked up from his own meal and smiled slowly. "Ah, yes," he said. "The chickens. Are you . . . ready to take them on?"

She chewed her lower lip. "I don't know," she said unhappily. "As I told Lester, I know nothing about them."

"Mm-hmm." He nodded. "I remember. I remember you almost turned green when he mentioned them. What's the matter, city girl? Afraid of a few little chickens?"

She bristled at his light sarcasm and set her fork down with a sharp click. "Of course I'm not afraid. But all I know about chickens is that they appear already cut into serving pieces in the supermarket. What do they eat? And when? And what else do I have to do for them except feed them?"

"Not much," he said, shrugging as he reached for the pot of chocolate to top off both of their mugs. "Chickens eat grain and mash, get fed twice a day, and have their water replenished at the same time. Whoever's in charge collects the eggs, and every now and then kills a couple of the older ones for stew."

Liss spurted a mouthful of hot chocolate back into her cup. "Kills?"

He nodded. "They get their heads cut off." He piled scrambled eggs onto a slice of toast and took a huge bite, chewing appreciatively. "You never heard of somebody running around like a chicken with its head cut off? They do, you know."

As her face went blank, he added, "Run around, I mean. After."

Liss looked down at her plate and knew she must be turning green all over again. Closing her eyes, she leaned back in her chair, then opened them again at the sound of a soft chuckle.

"Hey, don't pass out on me," Kirk said. "I was kidding. At least about your having to do that. I'm sorry," he added, stroking the backs of her fingers. She jerked her hand away, annoyed with his teasing, yet undeniably relieved there were no chickens.

"We don't keep chickens," he went on. "These eggs come from the farm across the river that forms our southwestern boundary—and so do the chickens you'll find in the deep freeze. Some are even cut up into serving pieces ready for you to cook."

Embarrassed that he'd gotten the better of her, Liss briskly changed the subject again. "What kind of schedule are you used to keeping? I mean, for meals, since I'll be in charge of them."

"What I'm accustomed to—though if it doesn't suit you, we can negotiate changes—is Monday through Friday, breakfast at six, right after I milk. Lunch when I get in from doing my chores around noon, and dinner somewhere between five-thirty and six-thirty. Weekends, at least this time of year,

I sort of let the schedule go and milk when I feel like getting up, unless the cow's bawling wakes me earlier."

Breakfast at six? she repeated silently. It was unbelievable to her that anyone would want to eat at that hour. She'd have to be out of bed by five-thirty at the latest. But . . . how early must he get up, in order to do the milking first? "How many cows do you have?"

"A couple of thousand head right now."

She gaped at him. "You milk two thousand cows before breakfast?"

It was his turn to gape. "No!" he said, and laughed as he spread strawberry jam on his toast. "This is a cattle ranch, not a dairy farm, city girl. I milk one cow for our personal use. We raise Simmental cows that we breed with Charolais bulls to produce beef. You know, roasts? Steaks? Hamburgers? The kind of stuff you find in the supermarket. It originates on the hoof."

"I know that." She reached for the jam.

"Of course you do. I'm sorry. I was teasing again."

"And I'm sorry to be so ignorant about ranch life," she said. "They don't teach a lot about cattle in art school."

"Art school?" He looked interested. "Are you an artist?"

"I have a master's in fine arts, and I do paint now and then, but my preferred medium is photography." She patted her smaller camera case, which sat on the chair at her side.

"I see," he said, then shook his head. "Actually no, I don't see." He remembered the dozen or so little kids who'd come rushing out of her tiny house when he'd stopped to pick her up and drive her to the lawyer's office. "If you're a photographer, why were you baby-sitting for a living?"

"It takes money to make money," she said sharply. It was a trite excuse, but in her case, it was true. Still, that was no reason for her to have snapped at him.

"Since my husband died," she went on in a softer voice, "I haven't done much photography. I do better with rural scenery and animals than weddings and graduations and baby portraits, which are about all I've been getting recently in the way of work." She didn't say that she thought she'd gotten those jobs because the people who'd hired her either couldn't afford a "real" photographer, or felt sorry for her and offered her the job—at a reduced rate because she didn't have a proper studio.

"I do—did—what in the trade is known as stock photography, selling my work freelance through an agent to people who produce calendars, inspirational books, greeting cards, and travel magazines. But . . . " She shrugged. "Last year when my washing machine broke down, I had to sell my best camera, and without photographs to sell I couldn't buy film or pay lab costs. Without equipment, I couldn't take photographs." She gave him the first genuine smile he'd seen since she'd arrived. It smacked him right in the solar plexus, as hard as it had the first time she'd aimed it at him a month ago.

"That's a problem I can empathize with " he said, struggling to keep his mind on the conversation and not on the memory of the incendiary kiss they'd shared. "We went through a bad spell a few years back and lost quite a bit of stock. Since we had less beef to sell, we didn't have the cash flow to

replace the lost stock. It took a while to recuper-
ate."

"Exactly," she said, "except for 'stock and beef'
substitute 'camera equipment and lab costs,' and
you have—are you going to hate me for this?—the
picture."

He laughed, and it was a sound Liss thought she
could get used to very, very quickly, just as she
could become accustomed to the glow in his eyes
when their gazes collided and clung for a heart-
stopping moment. She swallowed her last bite of
toast, drained her mug of hot chocolate, and
stood. Automatically, she began stacking dishes.
She wasn't quite sure where she'd put them once
they were stacked; she only knew that she had to
move. It was too risky sitting there looking at him.

Kirk stood also and opened the dishwasher,
which he began unloading. As he stepped aside
with a stack of clean dishes, she slipped in with a
pile of dirty ones. He glanced at her slender form,
her profile obscured by her thick dark hair, and
recalled the sagging gate outside her house in
Vancouver, the cracked sidewalk, the rough neighborhood. He'd known instinctively that she hadn't
belonged in that environment, that she'd been
there because circumstances had put her there.

"Things haven't been easy for you, have they,
Liss?" he asked, turning from setting the stack of
plates in a cupboard.

Liss shot him a sharp glance, but answered
easily. "It hasn't been too bad," she said with a
shrug and a deprecating smile. "I have two great
kids and we're happy together. That's what I find
important."

She finished loading the dishwasher with most
of the dishes that filled the sink, and he passed her
the box of detergent. After pouring the soap in, she

straightened, flipping her hair back, then turned to wipe off the plastic tablecloth.

Kirk watched her neat, deft movements as she swept crumbs into her hand and brushed them into the sink. It hasn't been too bad? he repeated silently. Who did she think she was kidding? He knew, better than most men, the trials of the single mother. On their way to pick up Mrs. Healey, she'd mentioned having once driven a taxi, and quitting only after she'd been robbed at gunpoint. She was a widow, that much he knew. Had her husband left her with nothing at all? He frowned, remembering the way her chin had lifted, the quick, sharp way she'd corrected Lester when he'd called her Mrs. McCall.

"I've never used my late husband's name," she'd said. "Please call me Liss, Liss Tremayne." The Liss, she'd explained, was short for Phyllis, another name she preferred not to use, since it was her mother's and it saved confusion at family gatherings. At the time, her pride and independence had somehow irritated him, even though he normally admired both characteristics. Did those attributes keep her from accepting help from her parents, he wondered, or were they also as poor as she appeared to be?

Liss cast a glance at Kirk's face as he filled the sink with water and started to wash the overload. He was familiar with the task of washing dishes, she could see. Yet she was troubled by the introspective look on his face. This couldn't be easy for him, sharing his house with two strangers, she thought as she started to dry. She had understood his shock at the will reading and believed he had a right to be angry—but with Ambrose, not with her. Then he'd calmed down and agreed to the terms of his father's will. Like Liss, and perhaps even Mrs. Healey, he'd had no choice.

"I never knew Uncle Ambrose," she said, "but I'm grateful for what he did, making it possible for my kids to have a better life. Can you tell me something about him?"

He glanced at her, his eyes unreadable, then turned his attention back to the dishes. "There's not much to tell. He was a big man, tall, broad shouldered, good-looking, I suppose, in a craggy sort of way, but stooped and thin toward the end." He gave Liss a crooked smile that lasted only a second. "He also had all his hair and most of his teeth and a low opinion of nearly everybody he ran into. I don't think you'd have liked him much."

She eyed Kirk's tall, broad-shouldered physique and his craggy face, and decided that he might have gotten his own good looks from his father. "Do you resemble him?"

He shrugged. "Maybe. Some. I have my mother's coloring. Brose was dark." His quick smile flashed again. "Every woman's dream, tall, dark, and handsome. Like my mother says, she fell for that, didn't see the personality that went with it, and paid the price."

Liss had wondered why Ambrose and Kirk's mother hadn't married. Now, she wondered if Ambrose had refused, even though the lady was pregnant. Kirk's age told her that his parents had known each other long before her aunt had come on the scene. "Where does your mother live?" she asked, and then cringed, wondering if maybe she no longer lived.

"Outside of Edmonton," he said to her relief, but his closed expression told her he didn't want to talk about that. "Your parents?" he asked. "Are they . . . ?"

"Alive?" She nodded. "Oh, yes. They split up when I was fourteen." He raised his head and his hands stilled in the water as he gave her a questioning look. She smiled brightly. "They both remarried almost at once and started new families, so I have plenty of little siblings running around. Some in Halifax, some in Kentucky. A couple of them are younger than Ryan."

He frowned. "Who did you stay with?"

She gave a half shrug. "I sort of went from one to the other and back again as was convenient."

Convenient for whom? Kirk wondered, but didn't question her on that. "How old are your kids?" he asked instead.

"Ryan will be five on January sixth, and Jason turns four exactly a month later. Do you have brothers and sisters?"

He shook his head, and they finished the rest of the dishes in silence. As she hung her wet tea towel over the oven door handle, he poured the rest of the hot chocolate into their mugs.

"Thank you," she said as she took her mug from him. "And thank you for this." She gestured at the much tidier kitchen. "I was dreading facing it in the morning." She glanced uneasily at the window where the snow still pelted. She was simply dreading morning. "Will this be over by then?"

He met her worried gaze with a sympathetic expression. "I can't tell. The system bringing it in is stalled over the mountains and we'll have to wait for it to move on." He reached into his pants pocket and pulled out her keys. "I put your car in the garage for you," he said, setting the keys on the table. "Even in the wilderness, it's a good idea not to leave the keys in the ignition. When the snow stops, I'll plow out the yard and the driveway, and the highway crews will be working all night to keep the main road open." He smiled faintly. "It won't snow forever, and the roads are normally clear."

"I know. It was fear talking when I said that."

"With reason. I'm sure this is the first blizzard you've ever experienced."

She nodded. "Of course, we get snow on the coast, but never this much. I'll get used to it, though." She sipped her chocolate. He didn't say anything more, and she started for the door, carrying her mug. "Well, then," she said awkwardly, "I'll say good night."

"Liss." She stopped, and he approached, coming to a halt only inches from her. "May I do it right this time?"

She frowned, too tired to figure out what he meant. "What?"

"This." He caught her chin, bent, and kissed her softly on the mouth. "Welcome to Whittier Ranch."

She swallowed the sudden thickness that sprang up in her throat. "Thank you," she whispered, then said again, "Good night."

Liss lay in bed listening to the howling wind. In spite of Kirk's welcome, she still felt alone, still shivered with doubts of what the future held. She slept restlessly that night, and when she awoke in the morning, the storm continued to rage indoors and out.

As she listened to Kirk arguing loudly with Mrs. Healey about her treatment of the dog, the boys scurried into her room, their eyes wide. They climbed in to chill her with their small, icy feet and warm her with their tight hugs. Jason giggled as Kirk bellowed something about how he didn't care how Brose had treated his animals, no dog of his got tied outside in a blizzard to repel nonexistent burglars.

"He's mad," Jason said, seeming impressed.

The slamming of a door echoed through the house, quickly followed by the sound of a loud engine starting as Kirk went about his "chores," whatever they might be, beyond milking the cow.

The storm continued all day while Liss unpacked their clothing and personal items and made their bedrooms truly their own with familiar and favorite objects she'd managed to cram into the back of the Blazer. Other things, including her furniture, would be delivered in a few days. She had a couple of encounters with Mrs. Healey, but mostly the older woman kept either to her bedroom or to the office until midafternoon. Of Kirk, there was no sign, and to her relief, he'd taken his dog with him wherever he'd gone.

She found one large, obviously unused room down the hall from the kitchen and decided—since Mrs. Healey objected to their presence in the living room, where she was trying to watch television— that it would be the boy's playroom. She took out the few pieces of lumber that were stacked there, cleaned it from top to bottom, put in the children's toys, books, and games, and plugged in the TV she'd brought from home. She considered lighting a fire on the hearth, but decided to hold off on that until she knew the chimney was safe.

With Ryan and Jason occupied there, she tackled the upstairs.

By the time night came and the boys were asleep, Liss was grateful to slide into her bed, satisfied with her day's work. Tomorrow, she'd take on the downstairs. With a huge yawn, she stretched, then curled into a ball and slept.

She didn't awaken until a shaft of sunlight

sliced into her room and dazzled her eyes. Leaping out of bed, she dressed quickly and went in search of the boys.

By the evidence she found in the kitchen, Kirk had come home sometime after she'd gone to sleep and was up again. Her sons were with him, judging by the absence of their outdoor clothing. She hurried through the utility room and snatched open the back door, then came to a sudden halt, gasping with delight as she stared at the scene surrounding her.

Her quick inhalation stung her chest with cold air as she looked at the sky arching overhead, a high, pure dome of blue. Here and there groups of tall, slender, leafless trees held delicate puffs of snow aloft, as if about to toss them into the air out of sheer exuberance. Mountains stood like a first line of defense on both sides of the flat, open valley with a silver river running its length. The inner defense, short, broad-based, dark-toned evergreens, stood stiffly at attention on the near side of the valley floor, wearing white busbies. Closer at hand and visible between the white trunks of poplars were several outbuildings and a pasture. A reddish-brown horse pranced through the snow in the pasture, tossing his long black mane and tail as he kicked up flurries. Liss's gaze swept back and forth as she mentally photographed each scene.

The clean cover of the yard was marred only by a line of footprints leading through the trees to the larger barn. From that direction came the sound of childish laughter and, to her shock, one deep-throated bark.

Coatless, bootless, Liss flew along the narrow track of footprints, snow gathering on the fuzzy material of her slippers. She coughed against the cold invasion of her lungs, her hand going to her throat even as she lunged through the door into the dimly lit, warm barn. Instantly spotting Jason, she snatched him away from the huge shaggy dog rolling with him in a pile of yellow straw. Holding Jason up and away from the animal, she backed toward the door. The dog stood up and grinned at her, tongue hanging out, head cocked to one side as if in question.

"Mom-mee," Jason protested indignantly. "He's a nice doggy. He likes me. I hug him."

The dog ambled over, licked Liss's hand, and she felt her legs turn to water. "Yes," she said, putting Jason back on his feet. "So I see. Sorry, Jase. I was a little worried when I heard him bark." One thing she didn't want to do was impart her own fear of dogs to her children. "Where is your brother?"

"Right here," Kirk said.

Liss whirled at the sound of his voice and saw him poking his head around a wall behind which he—and Ryan—were hidden. She walked around the wall, wondering what they could be doing. Under the light of a dangling bulb, Kirk sat on a low stool and milked a cow. At the sight of him— dressed in a thick green sweater, a down vest, and faded jeans, and clean-shaven—a jolt went through her not unlike the shock of the icy air. She tried to ignore it, but when he spoke again in that deep, soft voice of his, goose bumps raced over her arms and her stomach quivered.

"Good morning, Liss," he said, giving her a long look over his shoulder. The smile on his lips reminded her of how they'd felt on hers Friday night. She wished, suddenly, that she was wearing something other than the comfortable, faded yellow track suit she'd gotten in the early fall from Value Village, and of course, her shaggy slippers with little balls of ice clinging to their fake fur. His smile broadened, and she felt heat rising in her face. She was glad she stood with her back to the sunlit doorway so he couldn't see her clearly.

Ryan, crouched in the straw beside Kirk, could scarcely spare her a glance. "This is the milking parlor, Mom, and I'm gonna get a turn milking," he said importantly. "In just a minute. You want to watch?"

She did not. The very idea of her child going that close to an animal ten times his size made every one of her instinctive fears stand on end. "Um, I'm not sure that's such a good idea," she said quietly. She wanted to snatch him up as she had Jason, but what if a sudden move startled the cow and it lashed out with its feet? Cows were known to kick people. Even a city girl knew that. "You've never milked a cow before. You might . . . hurt it."

Kirk grinned as he swept another glance over Liss. Lord, but she packed a big wallop for such a little thing, he thought. Even dressed in baggy sweats, she was so shapely, he wanted to strip her clothes off and run his hands all over her. Would her body be the same creamy ivory color as her face? He swallowed hard and forced his mind back to the issue at hand. She was cute as a bug, but also scared to death of the cow. Her eyes were huge as she stared at it, and her white teeth gnawed on her lower lip. He nearly laughed at her statement— "*You might hurt it.*" It wasn't the cow she was afraid for, but her child.

Well, that was okay, he reminded himself. It was a mother's place to fear for her kids. Or so his mother had told him repeatedly when she'd thought he was about to do something dumb or dangerous or both.

"It's all right, Liss," he said in the calm, soothing voice he always used around cattle. "This is Coco.

She's very gentle. I promise she won't hurt your son, She's never hurt anybody in her life." The milk never stopped its rhythmic splashing against the side of the pail.

"Maybe not so far," she said, "but Ryan's never milked a cow. He might do something wrong, hurt her accidentally. And he's a stranger to her. How do you know she'll let a stranger touch her nip—uh—whatevers?"

Kirk's eyes laughed into hers for an instant. "Don't be anthropomorphic, Liss."

To her disgust, heat rose in her cheeks again. "I wasn't." But she knew she had been. Still . . . Stepping gingerly into the milking parlor, she reached out and took Ryan's hand, pulling him up. "Ry, come on, honey. Maybe you can learn to milk a cow when you're bigger." He pouted, about to argue, and she set her chin stubbornly. "Ryan. Now."

Kirk flicked another quick glance over her before returning his attention to the cow. Liss felt as if she'd been fully assessed and found not quite up to standard. "Do what your mother says, buddy," he said quietly.

Ryan, with uncustomary docility, went with Liss. With a silent sigh of relief, she was about to escape from the warm, dim building, with its odors of straw and animals, when a shadow filled the doorway. From out of the blinding sunlight came an apparition that made the big dog and the placid cow look like residents of the petting zoo.

With a squeal, Liss grabbed her children, one under each arm, and whirled. She darted back inside the milking parlor and flung herself at Kirk as an enormously tall horse stepped daintily into the barn.

Three

"Dammit," Liss said to herself a couple of hours later. Though she was nearly done cleaning the entire main floor, she was still steaming over her own idiotic behavior. "I wasn't scared," she assured herself. "I was merely startled. I didn't need him and his girlfriend laughing at me, making me look like a fool."

It hadn't been Kirk and Kristy Chandler who'd made a fool out of her, though, she had to admit. It had been herself. She would never forget the way Kirk's chest had vibrated with laughter as he'd gathered her and her armsful of children into a tight, protective embrace and spoken soothingly through his irrepressible chuckles. It was simply easier to try to blame them rather than herself. She had never flung herself into a man's arms in her entire life! At least not for that kind of reason.

Liss rammed the business end of the vacuum cleaner against the baseboard at the end of the hallway before turning and heading back the other way on her final pass. She remembered all too clearly Kristy Chandler's dancing green eyes, her tousled blond hair, and her giggle when Kirk scolded her for "scaring a poor city girl," as if the term were synonymous with "stupid."

She sniffed. "All right," she muttered, "so the cow didn't hurt Ryan, and yes, the dog turned out to be a nice, gentle animal that adores kids, and horses don't eat people now any more than they did when I was a child, but I didn't grow up here, riding horses and milking cows and spending weekends with Kirk Allbright on his damn ranch like that rosy-cheeked Kristy Chandler." She wondered why Kristy wasn't spending that weekend with Kirk, then cringed at the memory of Kristy's expression of disbelief when Kirk told her he couldn't go for a ride because he had to help Liss clean the house.

Kirk. A glance over her shoulder showed him hard at work in the living room, where bright sunshine lighted the place, revealing old but comfortable furniture, a scarred coffee table, and many bookcases stuffed with hardcovers, paperbacks, and journals. A Franklin stove, in which he'd built a fire, sent a steady, homey warmth through the room, in addition to that which came from the basement furnace. The boys were kneeling by the coffee table, coloring industriously in their books. Kirk had declared that the room she'd designated as their playroom was too cold until he could get carpet laid in there, and it wasn't comfortable with only floor cushions to sit on. Mrs. Healey would have to share the living room no matter how much she objected.

He looked up and saw her, and smiled that slow smile of his, the one that crinkled the corners of his eyes and creased his face. The one that made her insides quiver and her breasts tingle. He wielded a can of spray-on furniture polish and a rag, yet he appeared anything but domesticated. She wondered if he knew how good he looked, wondered if he knew how quickly and powerfully she responded to him. She flicked a glance over his broad shoulders, his narrow hips, and his long legs, and found herself flushing at the memory of the way he'd felt when he held her, so solid and strong and masculine. Swallowing hard, she turned her back on him, trying not to remember the feel of his mouth on hers. Of course he knew how she responded, she chided herself. By his own admission, plenty of women responded to him. She recalled the words he'd growled to Lester Brown, when he'd objected to having her and Mrs. Healey in "his" house.

"But I take them home on Sunday night and leave them there," she mimicked, "because I'm a bachelor and I like it that way."

"How come you're muttering at the vacuum cleaner?" Kirk asked from directly behind her. "Isn't it working right?"

Liss straightened abruptly and switched the vacuum off, finished at last. "It's working fine," she said, giving him and his furniture polish an unfriendly glance as he sprayed the arms of a wooden coatrack. "I wish you'd leave that alone and go and do some—some ranching, or something. I told you there's no need for you to do housework." She glanced at the stairs to see if Mrs. Healey was in sight. "If you-know-who catches you at it, she'll probably deduct your wages from my quarterly payment."

He grinned as he wiped the first arm of the rack, rubbing until it shone. "You let your son help me milk, so I owe you one."

She snorted. "Two little squirts of milk hardly constituted help, so go. Leave it. This is Sunday, isn't it, one of the days you reserve for your women?"

He stared at her, seeming undecided whether to laugh or scowl. "For my what?"

"Women," she explained earnestly. "You know, girlfriends like Kristy and whoever else there is? In Lester Brown's office you said you date nearly every weekend, but like to take them home on Sunday night and leave them there. I feel bad that my being here is interfering with your lifestyle."

Oh, for the love of Mike! Kirk thought. Trust a woman to remember, almost word for word, his largely exaggerated statement. "Don't you give my lifestyle another moment's consideration," he said, grinning. "I'm not complaining."

When her expression failed to soften, he sighed and said with careful patience, "Look, if we're going to live together in relative harmony, then we'll both have to make adjustments, Liss, and try to get along."

He turned back to the coatrack, working his way down its intricately carved base. Watching him, Liss knew exactly what "adjustments" he'd have to make. He was a nice man, and with a couple of little kids in the house, to say nothing of Mrs. Healey, whom Lester Brown had described as a chaperone, he wouldn't be able to bring his women home.

Mrs. Healey herself broke into her thoughts, coming down the stairs in a green satin robe that could have covered the roof of a stadium.

"Am I permitted to walk where you have vacuumed, miss?" she asked waspishly.

Liss bowed and swept her arm out. "By all means, please do, Mrs. Healey." The older woman sailed on by into the living room, where she ignored the children's greetings and turned the TV on to an evangelical program.

Kirk cocked his head to one side. "What was that all about?"

Liss had to laugh, albeit a trifle weakly. "It started earlier this morning. She came downstairs when I was halfway through washing the kitchen floor and ordered me to leave it and go make her bed, at once, so she could get back into it and be comfortable. And then I was to bring her four pieces of French toast, lightly browned, six slices of bacon, and a pot of coffee."

Kirk stared. "What did you do?"

Liss unplugged the vacuum and began winding up its cord. "What could I do? I laughed at her and told her I wasn't her servant. If she wanted to eat, she'd have to be downstairs at mealtimes and accept what I put before her. Otherwise, she could cook for herself and clean up afterward. She would have to wait for her breakfast, though, since the floor was wet and I didn't want her walking on it."

He laughed. "Good for you. And what did she do?"

"She tried to call Lester, but of course it's Sunday and she only got the answering service. Since then, she's been in her room." Liss frowned. "She still hasn't eaten."

Kirk tossed the spray can up and caught it as it came down. He tucked it under one arm, then put the other one over her shoulders, steering her, and the vacuum cleaner she wheeled, toward the utility room. "It won't hurt her to miss a meal or two." He shook his head ruefully. "Lord, what a creature she is. What are we going to do about her?"

Liss shrugged herself out from under his heavy-muscled arm and moved away, ostensibly to put the vacuum in its cupboard. "There's nothing we can do except put up with her."

"Oh, I don't know." He set the spray polish on a high shelf and tossed his rag into the laundry hamper. "Maybe we could stake her out on a snowdrift the way the Eskimos did with their old people."

"That's gruesome," Liss said, shuddering. Still, she was unable to suppress a grin at the picture the idea created in her mind: Mrs. Healey, green satin, and snow . . . Heavens, search-and-rescue aircraft would come zooming in from all directions thinking she was a distress signal! "And wasn't it the Indians," she went on, "who staked people out, only not their old folks, but their enemies? And they did it on anthills."

"That's even more gruesome," he said, "to say nothing of more tempting. We don't have any anthills, though, so we're stuck with snowdrifts." He grinned evilly. "Let's do it. You carry her outside while I go scout around for a snowdrift big enough to take her."

Liss laughed, and Kirk took a step closer, his big, hard body trapping her between the washing machine and the deep freeze. "I like the sound of your laughter," he said softly. "It makes me think of Ferris wheels and cotton candy and warm summer nights."

Liss couldn't say a word. She could only look at him, her breath caught, her heart hammering high in her throat. He touched her cheek with one finger, then drew it down to her chin and traced the scar there.

"What happened here?" he asked.

She managed to breathe. "A dog bit me when I was ten."

He circled the scar gently, and a weird sensation

tingled in the muscles and nerves at the base of her spine. "Ah. That explains your fear of Marsh. How did it happen?"

She smiled, and Kirk decided her smile was as beautiful to behold as her laughter was good to hear. As he slid his hand around to the back of her neck, he wondered why she would smile with such delight at the memory of an injury.

"I was running on Kits Beach," she said, "because the wind was blowing, the surf beating in, and I felt wild and free and happy. I was so excited by the weather, by my own incredible speed, that I didn't even see our neighbor's dog running beside me until I turned and tripped on him. He thought he was under attack and reacted instinctively, I suppose." Her smile faded. "Still, I've found it difficult to trust dogs since then."

"I can imagine." No wonder she'd shied away from Marsh Friday night. He'd been one frantic animal, chained outside in the blizzard, barking and snarling even at Kirk, but in protest, not anger. "The first time I saw this scar," he went on, "I thought it was sitting there begging me to kiss it. Did anybody kiss it better when it happened?"

Liss shook her head. "Of course not. I was all covered in blood and needed stitches and a tetanus shot."

He stroked the scar again with his thumb, and she was potently aware of how warm and strong his fingers were, and scented faintly with lemon oil. "And after that, did anyone?"

Wordlessly, her throat clogged with an emotion she didn't want to dwell on, she shook her head. Her heart beat with such incredible slowness that it hurt. Her knees were weak. Her eyelids felt heavy. Warmth curled through her belly and into her thighs.

"Then it's time, isn't it?" He bent down from his much greater height so that his face was near hers.

She splayed a hand on his chest. "Kirk . . . this isn't a good idea," she whispered huskily. He didn't agree, which was all right, because she wasn't absolutely sure she meant what she'd said, anyway.

His lips were as firm as she remembered. He kissed her scar, warmly and tenderly, then moved on up to her lips, catching her slight gasp so that it drew the taste of him into her mouth. His hand on the back of her neck flexed, and she tilted her head in response, opening herself to him with a shaky, trembling sigh. He swung his other arm around her, urging her onto her toes as she clung to his shoulders with both hands.

Moments later he lifted his head and slowly lowered her back to the floor. They stared at each other for a long, silent time, until she slipped under his arm and bolted.

Kirk let her go, although it was the last thing he wanted to do. He wanted to hold her, wanted to feel her heat, hear her breathing quicken.

"Be nice to her," Lester Brown had said. "You never know what might happen. You might even learn to like her."

Kirk pulled a face. Like her. Of course he'd probably learn to like her. Hell, he did already. Simply talking to her Friday night, starting to get to know her, had told him she was a likable woman. This morning, he'd learned he liked her quick wit and sense of humor. She didn't whine and complain, though he was certain she'd had a tough life since her husband died. But that didn't mean he had to lust after her. More important, it didn't mean he had to give in to Brose's hidden agenda. Dammit, he'd spent seven years fighting the old man on all sorts of levels, and mostly winning. Now, he was damned if he'd let him dominate from the grave. He knew exactly what Brose's will had been geared to force him into.

Marriage.

He jammed his feet into his boots, dragged his jacket on, and opened the back door. The cold cleared his head quickly after the warmth of the house—and the scent of the woman. She wasn't his type in any way, he told himself as he strode through the snow. What he had to do was forget about her altogether and stick to women who suited him better. Not only was she the wrong type and the wrong size, they lived in the same house and he'd never wanted a live-in lover before. He was a bachelor, just as Brose had been for most of his life, and that was the way he meant to keep it.

He kicked one of the big tires on the tractor and a clump of snow thudded down. He began brushing snow off the machine, then started the engine and drove it into its shed, where he should have put it Friday night. Friday night . . . Liss Tremayne . . . her bed behind him . . . Hell and damnation! Liss, in bed, was a thought he refused to dwell on. He was not taking her to bed.

He got off the tractor, flipped open the engine cover, and stared inside blindly. Liss Tremayne was a woman to stay the hell away from because he refused to play into Brose's hands.

He snatched up a wrench to tighten a bolt that wasn't loose. It slipped off the nut and his knuckles lost several square centimeters of skin. He cursed with undue fervor before sucking the sting out of them, then he heaved the wrench across the shed. It hit the plow blade with a satisfying clang.

• • •

"I'm going into town," Kirk said, after he'd finished the unnecessary monkey-wrenching on the tractor, and had showered and changed. "Is there anything I can pick up for you while I'm there?"

Liss looked up from the stove, where she was stirring soup. Kirk had changed from his ragged jeans and green sweater into a pair of newer jeans, equally tight, and a blue sweater that lightened the gray of his eyes. He was also wearing the inevitable cowboy boots and carried his hat in his hand. He looked just as good as he had half an hour before.

She forced herself to concentrate on his question. Hadn't she spent the past thirty minutes telling herself to quell her foolish attraction to this man? Of course she had. It was time she listened to her own words of wisdom. "Yes, please. Fresh fruit—apples, bananas, oranges, whatever you can get—and some carrots and onions."

"And some chocolate," Ryan said, grinning up at Kirk from where he knelt by the box of kittens. Mama cat now purred contentedly while the children played with her babies.

Liss scowled at him. "Ryan! You aren't supposed to ask for things."

"But Grandpa always brings us chocolate when he goes to the store," Ryan said.

Liss clenched her teeth. That was all too true. "Kirk is not your grandpa."

"Is he going to be our daddy?" Jason asked. "If he was our daddy he could bring us chocolate even if you said no 'cause daddies are the boss. Grandpa said so."

Liss groaned and covered her face with her hand, wishing she could drown out Kirk's chuckle with a shriek. "Hey, I like your attitude, kid," he said. "And your grandpa sounds like my kind of guy."

"Yeah," Jason said. "'Cept he and Grandma won't let us bring our bikes to our house. They make us keep them at their house and we only get to ride them when we go to visit. If you were our daddy could we have bikes here?"

Liss cringed. "Jason! I told you that maybe if you're really good, Santa Claus will bring you and Ryan bikes for Christmas. But if you're not good, you might not get anything. And being good means not asking for things."

"Hey, lighten up, Liss," Kirk said. "Asking for a chocolate bar isn't exactly a capital crime."

She glared at him. "Go shove your head in a bucket of water," she muttered, then added to Jason, "When I say no chocolate, I mean no chocolate, and that's that."

"Please? Let me get them some," Kirk said quietly. "I liked chocolate when I was a kid, too. Heck, I still like it. I'll pick up a couple of candy bars for them, okay? I really don't mind."

"But I do," she said, her tone just short of a shout. "Be good enough not to interfere with my decisions about what's best for my children. One of my prime reasons for agreeing to come live in this godforsaken snow-covered wilderness was so I could raise my sons without somebody else trying to undermine me and turn them into whining, demanding little brats who think the world owes them a living!"

He stared at her for a moment, then a closed look came over his face. He nodded curtly. "Sure. Right. Whatever you say."

She sighed, knowing she had sounded shrewish and mean, but seeing no graceful way out of it. All it had taken to turn her into a virago was the painful reminder that her children's grandparents tended to give them whatever they wanted—at their house—in order to pressure Liss into moving back in with them. She didn't need that kind of interference, and for a moment it had appeared that Kirk was doing it, too.

"How about some yogurt?" she asked, and the kids agreed happily. To Kirk, she added, "Half a dozen little tubs of fruit-flavored yogurt, too, please."

For a moment, he looked as rebellious as the boys had seconds before, but then he shrugged and jammed his hat on. Liss hated to see him leave like that, thinking she was a bad-tempered snark. She wasn't sure why it mattered so much, but it did.

"I'm going to have lunch on the table in five minutes," she said. "Will you eat before you go?"

Kirk felt that smile of hers sneak up on him and give him a hard zap in the gut. He took a step back, wondering how he had gotten so close to her. He hadn't been aware of moving, and she still stood where she'd been when he entered the room, a big white apron tied around her slim middle, her cheeks flushed from the heat. The soup smelled good. She smelled good. He wanted to touch her again so bad, he had to clench his hands into fists.

"No," he said roughly, turning on one heel and putting space, lots of it, between them. "I'll be late. Don't expect me for dinner, either," he added impulsively, without the faintest idea of where he'd eat. He only knew he had to escape before he kissed the living daylights out of Liss Treymayne in front of her little boys.

He plunged outside and drew in a deep breath of the icy air. It stung his nose and made his chest ache, but he took another breath, and another, until he had a damned good reason for the dizziness that assailed him. "Damn you, Brose," he muttered, getting into his truck and slamming the door.

"If you didn't go to hell, that's where you belong, the Reverend Daisy notwithstanding. What have you saddled me with? And how am I going to deal with it?"

There was no answer, of course. He started his truck and drove out of there as if something were chasing him. Damn right he was going to be late, he reaffirmed to himself. Maybe he wouldn't go home all night. That, he knew, was the most sensible course, but he still felt as if he were being hounded out of his own house.

He pounded his fist on the steering wheel. Dammit, whose ranch was this, anyway?

"That is my place," Mrs. Healey said, tapping Liss on the shoulder with a stiff, hard finger. "Ambrose sat at that end, I sat at this one."

Liss jerked around, staring up at Mrs. Healey. *Dammit,* she thought, *for a large woman, Mrs. Healey could move awfully quietly when she chose not to hammer her cane on the floor at each step.* Though Liss had called a few minutes before to alert her that lunch was ready, there had been no response. Now that she and the boys were nearly done, here came the silent mountain, sneaking up on her.

"Excuse me," she said with exaggerated courtesy. "I had no idea this was your special place." At lunch and dinner the day before, Mrs. Healey had come in, filled a plate, then disappeared with it, either to her room or to the office. Now, it seemed, she had decided to join the family. "I'll be happy to

sit elsewhere at dinnertime and from then on-
ward," Liss continued. "But for now, please sit at
the other end of the table, Mrs. Healey, and help
yourself to lunch." She indicated the pot of soup
on the stove and the plate of sandwiches on the
table. "Unless, of course, you'd like to wait until
I've finished; then you'll be welcome to this seat."

With a "Hmmph" and a toss of her head, the
older woman grudgingly did as she was asked,
sitting down with a thump.

"Can we go now, Mom?" Ryan asked. He shoved
his bowl away and left a half-eaten triangle of
sandwich on his plate. "You said we could build a
snowman right after lunch."

"Yes, you may go. And help your brother with his
boots." Both boys scampered into the back entry
room, where she could hear them struggling with
snowsuits and boots.

She was about to go help when a female voice
called from the front hall. "Yoo-hoo! Kirk, darling,
where are you?"

The sound of that voice stilled both Mrs. Healey's
spoon halfway to her mouth and Liss in her tracks.
They turned to see a tall redheaded woman stride
into the kitchen on snowy boots, the smile on her
face dying the instant she saw the strangers.

"Oh!" Her glance, the same shade of blue as a
winter sky and about as warm, swept over Liss.
"Where is Kirk? And who are you?"

"Kirk is out," Liss said. "He may be late. I'm Liss
Tremayne." She squared her shoulders and reminded herself she had as much right to be there,
more even, than the newcomer, though the redhead clearly felt welcome to walk in unannounced
without even wiping her feet.

Jason came staggering back into the kitchen,
mittens dangling, asking to be zipped. Liss com-

plied, then did the same for Ryan. "These are my children," she went on to the other woman, "Ryan and Jason. And this is—"

"No need to introduce this lady." The redheaded woman strode right past Liss, failing utterly even to look at the boys, and offered her hand to Mrs. Healey. Smiling, she bent impulsively to kiss her cheek. "You must be Kirk's mother. He said you'd be coming to stay. How wonderful to meet you at last. He's told me so very much about you. I'm Gina."

She said it, Liss thought, as if the mere name would explain everything.

"I'm sure Kirk has told you all about me," Gina went on. Pulling out a chair, she sat close to Mrs. Healey, who so far hadn't said a word. She only sat staring, her mouth slightly ajar. With a tiny grimace, Gina added confidingly, "He's probably mentioned our little spat, too, but I'm here to make up." She laughed lightly. "Tell me, Mrs. Allbright, do you think he's ready to listen to reason now?"

Mrs. Healey finally closed her mouth and said, "I'm Mrs. Healey and I'm not his mother. I'm his coheir."

Gina's smile faded instantly. "Are you saying Kirk isn't sole heir to Whittier Ranch? But why? I mean, what were you to the old goat—to Ambrose?"

Mrs. Healey, Liss was perversely pleased to see, didn't reserve her bad manners and ill humor strictly for her housemates. "That," she said, shifting away from Gina, "can hardly be considered your business, and since this is my home now as well as Kirk Allbright's, I'll thank you not to enter without knocking another time."

"I . . . of course," Gina said, suddenly humble. "Forgive me, please, but I naturally had no idea . . .

and I'm accustomed to coming and going as if this were my own home. You see," she added in a sweet, little-girl voice that was completely at odds with her statuesque figure, "I expected that it would be my home by now, but when Ambrose got sick, Kirk . . . changed. I think it was grief that did it." Gina laid one long-fingered, red-nailed hand on Mrs. Healey's arm. "Please, won't you help me? I do love him so very much, but like most men, he can be terribly unforgiving at times. Mrs. Healey, I'm begging you, make him listen to me. That's all I ask, just that he listen to me! I truly wasn't trying to lure him away from his ranch. I'd be happy to live here year-round."

Mrs. Healey pulled her arm free, her expression one of distaste. "I have no influence over that young man, miss, nor do I want to. He's as rude, boorish, and insensitive as his father was. You're better off without him."

She turned and fixed a look of dislike on Liss. "And that," she added, "is advice you'd do well to heed, too, young woman, if you're tempted to do any more smooching in the laundry room. That boy is his father all over again, using sex and charm and empty promises to keep a housekeeper around rather than paying her a living wage."

Quickly Liss shooed the boys out the back door, wondering what Mrs. Healey had seen and heard. Gina's cold gaze swept over Liss for the second time. "You and Kirk, smooching in the laundry room? I can tell you one thing, when Kirk and I are married, there'll be no need for a housekeeper, so don't get too comfortable."

Liss gritted her teeth and forced herself to keep her hands and her tongue out of mischief. Nothing would be gained by deliberately antagonizing this woman, regardless of how antagonistic she was toward her. But, Liss reflected, that didn't mean she had to take any abuse, either.

"I hope you'll both excuse me," she said calmly. "I don't like to leave the children outside alone too long. Good-bye, Gina. Nice meeting you."

"My name," Gina said pointedly, "is Miss Holland."

The silence, as Liss walked briskly out of the kitchen and into the back room, was almost palpable. When she returned from outside more than an hour later, after she and the boys had built a marvelous snowman, she was not surprised to see that the table had not been cleared and the soup pot still stood on the stove. From the living room she heard the hum of a low-voiced conversation. Mrs. Healey and Gina Holland, it seemed, had struck up an unlikely friendship. Or was it, Liss wondered, hanging up her coat and the boys' outdoor gear, so unlikely? After all, both would be happier if Liss didn't exist. Maybe they thought that, together, they could force her to leave.

She tucked the boys into bed for a nap, then baked a chocolate cake to make up for being so stubborn over the candy bar issue. The cake was cooling, dinner was in the oven, and Liss was in the back entry hall, reaching up to a high shelf where she'd seen icing sugar stored, when Kirk came home.

"Oh!" Startled, she dropped down from her tip-toes and whirled around as he and Marsh came through the back door. Marsh's claws clicked on the tile as he walked over to her. He nudged her with his cold, wet nose, then continued on to the kitchen and his water dish, where he lapped noisily.

Kirk halted just inside the door and gazed at her, a defensive expression on his face, a stubborn thrust to his chin.

Her heart rate increased and her insides seemed to melt. She stiffened and said, "Hello. I thought you weren't coming home until late."

He set a grocery bag on the freezer, then banged the snow off his boots onto the mat by the door. His stare challenged her. "I changed my mind. This is my home, too, and I won't be forced out of it."

Liss's eyes narrowed. "I wasn't aware of having forced you out."

"You didn't," he said. Abruptly, he reached out and caught her around the waist, his cold hands startling on her bare skin, for her shirt had hitched up as she'd stretched for the sugar. "This did."

"What—" she started to say, but something in his expression silenced her. His eyes glittered under the brim of his hat. His chest rose and fell within the open front of his jacket. His powerful thighs brushed against hers, and his long fingers flexed on her waist, stroking the skin of her back. He bent low, held her tight against him, and then he kissed her.

Four

What the hell are you doing? Kirk asked himself as Liss's warm, soft lips parted instinctively under his.

Oh, hell, he was doing what he'd been wanting to do, what he'd been thinking about incessantly since he drove away at noon. No, dammit, he'd been thinking about it since this morning, since Friday night, since . . . since the first time he ever saw Liss Tremayne. He was out of his mind. He shouldn't have touched her. He'd told himself he wouldn't, just as he'd told himself to get out of the house and stay out until he had his libido back under control. But there he was, back home, touching her, kissing her, lifting his head and rubbing away the crick in his neck, then bending to kiss her again.

"Ah, Liss . . ." he said softly when he eased away for the second time. "You taste so good." She stared at him, her eyes bemused, and he knew he wasn't through with kissing her, no matter how bad it made his neck hurt. With a groan, he lifted her up and set her on the deep freeze, then stood

erect now that she was on a level with him. Both
hands cupping her face, fingers sliding into her
hair, he kissed her again deeply, his tongue probing, hers answering. Their hearts hammered rapidly, and both gulped for air when they finally
broke apart.

"I kept thinking," Kirk murmured, "about how
you tasted this morning, how you felt in my arms.
I wondered if it would still be the same." He
stroked a finger down her face until it rested on
the small scar on her chin. "My memory didn't lie,
but this time was better." He grinned. "Now, you
taste like chocolate."

"Oh."

"I like the taste of chocolate."

"So you . . . so you said."

He smiled. "May I have another taste?"

Liss swallowed hard, fighting the sensual pull of
his touch, his soft, seductive voice. She wouldn't
let herself be swayed by either, she vowed.

"No," she said.

"Liss . . ." He stroked one thumb over her moist,
red lower lip. Her eyes, shadowed, ever changing,
were mysterious, so alluring he wanted to go on
watching their varying expressions forever. He
caressed her lips again and watched the luminosity of those fantastic eyes intensify. Her lips trembled and she tried to turn her head aside, but his
hands held her still as he gazed at her. "If you won't
let me kiss you again, at least let me look at you."
Then in a rough whisper, he blurted out what he
was thinking before considering how it would
sound. "Lord, Liss. If a kiss makes you glow like
that, what must a climax do?"

He saw shock flood her eyes and instantly regretted his blunt words. She blinked and, in that short
moment, dispersed the unearthly radiance their

kiss had generated. "You . . . louse!" she gasped. "Let me go!" She jerked free, swinging her legs up and around him, and slid off the freezer even as he tried to stop her.

"Hey, come on," he said, blocking her path. "How come I'm suddenly a louse? What did I do that was so terrible? I kissed you, for the love of Mike! It wasn't against your will. You kissed me back. I'm sorry if I was out of line, mentioning a climax, but if you think kisses like that don't lead to lovemaking, you're wrong."

Where are your brains? Liss castigated herself. *One of this man's lovers had been there that morning; yet another was in the living room now, doubtless conspiring with Mrs. Healey to get rid of her. And there she was in the pantry letting him kiss her, kissing him back, listening to talk of climaxes and lovemaking and . . . Lord! In less than forty-eight hours, how had she managed to get herself into such a situation?*

"Lovemaking?" she said scathingly, as much to convince herself as to convince him. "Not between you and me, they don't."

"Why not? I'm a man. You're a woman. We're both well past the age of consent, and believe me, a kiss like that suggests consent."

"In your dreams! You said yourself," she went on before he could get a word in, "that we have to try to share this place in some kind of harmony, and we won't if you come on to me whenever you feel like a cheap thrill. So keep your kisses for other women. I don't want any part of them."

"Don't you? You did only moments ago."

"Because you took me by surprise," she defended herself. "But I have a surprise for you. Another of your girlfriends is here."

He frowned as he stepped back, setting her free. "Who?"

Liss laughed. She scooped up the bag of groceries, dropped the sugar box into it, and said over her shoulder as she headed into the kitchen, "Does it matter?"

Kirk felt overheated and disgruntled as he followed her. "Of course it matters." *Who in hell did Liss Tremayne think was his girlfriend?* he wondered. He sat on a chair at the end of the table to pull off his boots. It had been several months since he'd had anyone who could have been even remotely considered a girlfriend. Since long before Ambrose's death he simply hadn't had time.

"Hello, darling." He felt suddenly sick as he heard Gina speak in the doorway behind him. "I thought I heard your voice." He spun around, knocking over his boots as he shot to his feet.

"What the hell—" he began, but her mouth covered his, cutting off his words. He stood there, shocked into immobility, watching Liss's face freeze before she turned her back. He wrenched Gina off him and held her away from him, staring at her, searching for words powerful enough to get through this woman's thick, impervious skin. She was totally unable to believe him when he said something was over, and what had been between them was damned well over.

He was still gaping at Gina, wondering at her gall, when she reached over and poked Liss on the arm. "Would you get out of here?" she said. "Mr. Allbright and I would like a little privacy. Can't you find something else to do? Maybe the downstairs bathroom could do with a good cleaning. The last time I was here it was—"

"Gina!" Both Gina and Liss jumped at his loud voice. His hand whipped out to capture Gina's wrist, and he spun her back toward him. "Who the hell do you think you are, and who do you think you're talking to?" he demanded, his eyes dangerously cold. Liss thought if a look like that had been trained on her, she'd have shriveled where she stood. Gina, however, withstood it well.

"Now, Kirk, darling," she cooed, "Mrs. Healey explained everything to me. I know how little experience you have in dealing with inside help, so why don't you permit me to lay down some ground rules for, um, Lisa or whatever her name is? That way, things will be so much easier for . . . everyone."

"Such as whom?" Kirk asked in an ominously quiet tone.

"Such as you," she said, patting his cheek. "And dear Mrs. Healey." She hesitated for a second, then pouted prettily. "And me, darling, because I simply can't live without you and I know that in your heart of hearts you really do want me to move in with you and—"

"Move *in* with me? Gina, all I want is for you to get out of this house!"

"But—"

"But nothing!"

Taking her arm, Kirk inexorably led Gina toward the front door, apparently knowing without having to ask that she had come in that way. Of course, Liss thought, turning so she could watch their progress down the hall through the kitchen doorway. Gina Holland was not the back-door type.

"I may not have much experience dealing with 'inside help,'" he went on, "which Ms. Tremayne is not, but I have plenty of experience in throwing you out when you assume too much and won't take no for an answer."

Gina wriggled free and faced him. "But, Kirk, you don't mean—"

"Dammit!" he roared, flinging her caressing hand off his cheek. "I mean exactly what I say! I've played this scene with you a few times too many, Gina, and I'm getting sick of it!" He put his hands on her upper arms and marched her in front of him toward the door.

Mrs. Healey came out of the living room in response to Kirk's words and Gina's whining protests. "Young man," she exclaimed, "what is the meaning of this? Why are you manhandling that poor girl? Let her go at once."

As Liss watched in fascination, Kirk let Gina go, but only to grab her jacket off the coat tree he'd polished so hard that morning. He held it out to Gina, waiting. "Hardly manhandling, Mrs. Healey," he said. "I'm simply escorting an unwelcome, uninvited guest to the door. Kindly keep out of it. Gina, put your coat on."

"What do you mean, unwelcome and uninvited?" Mrs. Healey said. "I welcomed Gina. I invited her. In fact, she's joining us for dinner. Isn't that right, my dear child?"

"Thank you, Olga," Gina said, simpering, then appealed to Kirk again. "See, darling? I'm staying."

The high heels of her black boots made her almost as tall as Kirk, Liss noticed, and wondered how Gina still managed to look frail and delicate. She'd never before seen anyone with a D-cup look delicate. Come to think of it, she'd never believed there was a man alive who'd willingly throw out a woman who wore a D-cup. Maybe this romance of Gina's *was* all on one side.

She stroked his face again with her long-fingered hand, and he again shook it off. "Please, darling," she said, "don't be angry with me anymore. I didn't mean to hurt your little housekeeper's feelings. I'll be good. Just as good as gold. I promise, Kirkie."

Liss couldn't quite stifle her spurt of laughter. *Kirkie?* "Yes, do let her stay, Kirkie," she said, leaning against the door frame. "It's a big roast."

He turned on her, his eyes blazing. "You keep out of this!" Wheeling back to Gina, he said, "I don't care who invited you. You aren't welcome and—"

"She is welcome and she's staying. As my guest," Mrs. Healey said, putting a protective arm around Gina. "Come along back into the living room, dear child," she continued, looking, Liss mused, like a rotund dachshund escorting an Irish wolfhound. "We won't let this boorish man deny us our friendship."

Before the two went three paces, however, the front door swung open. Didn't anybody knock in this neighborhood? Liss wondered, then blinked in surprise as Kristy Chandler strode in, brushing snow off her jeans, then shaking her blond hair loose as she snatched off her red wool cap.

"My goodness!" she exclaimed, coming erect. "What smells so good in here?"

"Roast beef," Liss said, grinning as Kristy saw Gina and did a wonderful double take. Liss sat down on the bottom step of the staircase to watch what she was certain would be exciting fireworks. "Why don't you stay for dinner?"

Kirk let out a strangled sound as he turned to her, signaling silently with frantic gestures of eyebrows and mouth.

Kristy gazed speculatively at Gina. "What are you doing here? I thought you were a thing of the past."

"I," Gina said, "am not a 'thing.'" She sniffed

disdainfully. "And speaking of past history, what makes you think there's anything here for you?"

Kristy grinned. "Well, there's dinner, for one thing." The smile she gave Gina was so cheerfully malicious that Liss decided she liked the blonde. This situation was funny, and if both women stayed, she thought it might get even funnier. She could do with a good laugh.

"Thanks, Liss," Kristy continued. "I accept your dinner invitation, although what I came for was to invite you to bring your children to my place for riding lessons next Saturday."

Gina turned to Kirk, her hand on his arm. "Darling, please, why don't you and I drive into town for dinner? If we had only a little time together, a few moments of privacy, I know I could show you how wrong you are. I know you need me now as you never did before and—"

This time, the door didn't open without warning, but Gina broke off at the sound of something thudding against the wood panels. With an impatient sigh, Kirk broke free of Gina again and jerked the door open to admit yet another redhead. Putting a hand over his eyes, he groaned loudly and would have turned to go, but the newcomer crowded close to him, raised up on tiptoes, and kissed him on the cheek.

"Mmm, you smell delicious," she said, oblivious of the others standing around. She carried a covered dish and thrust it at Kirk, saying "Take this, will you, hon?" before removing her glasses, which had fogged the instant she stepped into the warm house. Casually she lifted Kirk's sweater and tugged his shirttail out of his pants to wipe the steam off her lenses. Liss watched, amazed as Kirk stood there holding the casserole and staring at the ceiling as if he wished he were anywhere else.

Clearly this woman was quite accustomed to un-dressing Kirk Allbright and didn't mean to let an audience deter her.

"Hello, Gina," the short redhead said, peering nearsightedly as she rubbed her glasses. "Fancy meeting you here, cousin. I thought you were a thing of the past."

"I'm not a—" Gina began, but the newcomer, putting her glasses back on again, spotted Kristy.

"Oh, my. Are we having a fan club reunion, ladies, or is this the play-offs?" Without waiting for a reply, she turned to Mrs. Healey and greeted her by name.

"Remember me?" she asked Mrs. Healey. "I'm Patty Fontaine, Alice and Frank's daughter. I was probably only about thirteen the last time you saw me, so I'm sure I've changed, though you haven't, not one bit. Anyway, my mom asked me to drop by with that casserole as a welcome-back offering and to tell you how happy she is to learn that you've returned to the valley. She says Tuesday morning quilting club hasn't been the same without you and hopes you'll be along this week."

Pausing, Patty sniffed long and appreciatively. "My goodness! I think I'd forgotten how wonder-fully you used to cook, Mrs. Healey. Something smells heavenly in here." She grinned at Kirk. "Besides you."

Kristy laughed. Gina made an angry sound.

"It's roast beef," Liss said, getting to her feet. She introduced herself, then added, "Won't you stay for dinner? We seem to be collecting a party here."

Before Patty had a chance to accept or decline, yet another knock sounded, this one at the back door. Liss, with a questioning glance at Kirk, went to answer it.

"Hello," said the middle-aged lady who stood

there, her glasses fogging as quickly as Patty's had. "I'm Daisy Crandall, rector of St. John's Church." She peered at Liss through the fog. "Are you Olga Healey?"

"No," Liss said, "but she's here. Please, come in."

She steered the half-blind minister through the kitchen and into the front hall where the others remained. Kirk's head was swinging back and forth as he monitored a lively argument between Gina and Kristy.

"Mrs. Healey," Liss announced, "this is the Reverend Daisy Crandall."

"My dear Olga." Reverend Daisy mistakenly grabbed Kristy's hand and pumped it vigorously. "I am delighted to meet you." Deftly, Kristy turned the minister in the right direction. "I am rector of the church Ambrose attended the last few years of his life, and when I heard after the service today that you had arrived, I knew I must come and welcome you, and invite you to our Wednesday night prayer meeting and the ladies' guild on Thursday morning." While Daisy talked, Patty lifted the minister's glasses from her face, wiped them on Kirk's shirttail, then replaced them without the cleric's missing a beat. "Ambrose told me so much about you. Welcome to the valley. My, my, something smells wonderful in here. Ambrose mentioned that you are a superb cook. What *are* you having for dinner?"

"The whole damned community," Kirk muttered.

"It's roast beef," Liss said, smiling mischievously at him. "We'd be delighted to have you join us."

"Good Lord," Kirk said, sotto voce. "Do you want me to go and slaughter another steer before I slaughter you?"

Liss laughed, enjoying herself more than she had in a long time. This would teach him to spread his kisses around indiscriminately. Talk about chickens coming home to roost! "There's no need to slaughter anything. As I said, it's a big roast."

Just then, Jason came stumbling down the stairs rubbing his eyes. "Mommy," he said. "I had a dream."

"So did I," Kirk said, shoving the casserole into Liss's hands. "A dream of peace. A dream of quiet. A dream of a winter's solitude." He jammed one hand through his thick hair. "Where did it go?" he asked of no one. "What happened to it?"

"Hi, Mom," Ryan said, bounding down the stairs. "Mmm. What smells so good?"

"Roast beef," said several people.

"And chocolate cake," Jason said. " 'Member? Mom promised."

Kirk, poised in the doorway between the hall and the kitchen, braced his hands on the door frame as if to hold himself back. "Chocolate cake? Chocolate *cake*? No!" he said firmly as if someone were begging him to stay. "No damn way! I'm out of here!" He strode through the doorway and a few seconds later the back door slammed. Hard.

Everyone had just sat down at the table, a strange and hardly compatible group, Liss thought, when Kirk returned. He stood at the threshold of the big, warm kitchen, his gaze sweeping over the group before settling on Liss.

She raised her brows. "I thought you were leaving."

He shoved his hat back. "I left," he said, scowling at her. Then, when no one spoke, he added, "I came back." He sounded as if he couldn't quite believe it himself.

"Darling," Gina said, getting up and going to

him. She lifted his hat off and patted his cheek. "I'm glad you did. Just as soon as dinner is over, you and I are going to have that little chat."

He grasped her wrist, pulled her hand away, and dropped it as he might a wet towel. After politely escorting her back to her chair, he removed his jacket and boots while Liss collected a place setting for him.

"Thanks, Liss," he said, as she set a plate and cutlery at the head of the table. He helped himself to roast beef, potatoes, gravy, and vegetables. "Mmm. This is what I came back for," he added, smiling wickedly at her as she resumed her seat between her sons. Holding her gaze with his, he ran his tongue over his lips and said softly, "This, and the taste of chocolate."

Deep inside Liss a throbbing began, and she looked quickly down at her plate. Dammit, she thought, she was not going to become number four on his list, or ten or twenty or anything, and he was not going to use her to keep the unwanted ones at bay.

When the last crumbs of chocolate cake had been scraped off plates, Kirk leaned back, looking satisfied.

"Wonderful," he said. "Thank you, Liss."

"You're welcome. Would anyone like more coffee?"

"Kirk and I will have some," Gina said, pushing back her chair. "You can bring it into the living room for us."

"Not a chance," Kirk said. "If you want more coffee, you'll have it while you clear the table."

Gina lifted her imperious nose. "While I do what?"

"You heard me," he said pleasantly.

Gina turned to Liss and gave her a sweeping, appraising stare that, after the assessment was complete, became dismissive. Facing Kirk again, she said, "I beg your pardon, but what would *she* be doing if I were to clear the table?"

"Taking a well-deserved break. Who do you think cooked all that food you pigged out on?"

"I," Gina said, "did not 'pig out' on anything."

Patty stood and rubbed her stomach. "Well, I certainly did. That was a great meal, Liss, and even if Kirk hadn't suggested it, I was prepared to clean up by way of saying thanks. I'll scrape and rinse if you'll load the dishwasher, Kristy. Come on, cousin, dear," she said to Gina. "It won't break your pretty nails to clear a table for once in your useless life." She shook her head. "And to think you imagine yourself as a rancher's wife."

"But I'd make a won— Kirk! Where are you going?"

He smiled as he tugged on his jacket. "I'm going to milk."

"Then I'll join you," Gina said.

"Can I come, too, Kirk?" Ryan asked.

"Sure," he said with almost laughable eagerness as Gina, with a petulant huff, subsided back into her chair. Kirk gave Liss a guilty look. "Unless your mother objects?" His eyes begged her not to.

"It's okay," Liss said to her son, far more because she knew he loved "helping" adults than because she wanted to let Kirk hide behind him. "But come in as soon as the milking is done. You're going to follow your brother right into the tub."

Gina and Kristy were gone by the time Liss had Jason bathed and came downstairs looking for Ryan. Patty was just finishing up in the kitchen, and Liss suspected she'd gotten stuck with the

entire job. "Thanks," she said with sincere grati-
tude. "The kitchen looks great."

"My pleasure." She gave Liss a friendly smile.
"But I have to be getting on home now. It's snowing heavily again." She picked up the dish she'd
brought, emptied now of its delicious zucchini-
tomato casserole, which they'd enjoyed with dinner. "I like your children, Liss," she added. "Are
you interested in putting either or both of them in
preschool? I teach first and second grades at the
local elementary, but there's a nursery group as
well, and joining it would be a good way for your
kids to make friends in the area. There are none
their age living very near this ranch."

As Liss walked the younger woman to the front
door, she considered that there were no people of
any age living what she would call "very near" the
ranch. All she said, though, was "Thanks. I'll give
it some thought."

It really was snowing hard, she saw as Patty left.
So much for the bright sunshine she'd enjoyed
that day and anticipated for tomorrow. As she
shut the door, she glanced at her watch. It was
long past time Ryan should have been in bed.
She'd have to go out and get him. To the barn. To
where Kirk was. She forcibly calmed the butterflies
in her stomach, put on her coat and boots, drew in
a deep breath, and stepped outside.

"You hold it like this," Kirk was saying as he and
Ryan bent over something. They were sitting on a
bench in a snug little room between the milking
parlor and the vast remainder of the calving barn.
Their backs were to the doorway, and she heard
Kirk continue, "Then ease it ahead, always away

from you, never toward you, and turn your wrist a little bit. Yes, that's it! Good boy!"

"Will I be able to make things like you do?" Ryan asked, and Liss's heart ached at the adoring look in his eyes as he gazed at the man.

"Sure you will."

"Will you teach me other stuff, too, so I can look after the ranch when I'm big?"

"You bet, buddy. If you're going to grow up to be a rancher, you'll need to learn lots of things." Kirk's smile was nothing short of tender as he brushed Ryan's hair back from his brow, and for a moment Liss felt like an intruder into something very special, very masculine. A male bonding maybe, which she, as a woman, shouldn't witness.

"When will I be able to do it like you do?" Ryan asked. "Soon?"

"Well, maybe not right away," Kirk said, "but in a year or two you'll be making lots of different things. I didn't start till I was older than you, so you'll probably learn faster than I did."

"Learn what?" Liss asked, stepping into the room.

"Whittlin'," Ryan said, turning to beam at her. An enormous knife was clenched in one very small fist, a piece of wood in the other. "Look, Mom!" He waved both stick and knife. The blade gleamed in the light shining down from overhead. "Kirk said I could."

Liss closed her eyes for a second and shuddered. If this was what male bonding was all about, she was glad she'd interrupted! "I . . . see. Ryan, give the knife back to Kirk, very, very carefully."

He did. "Now pull up your hood, zip your jacket all the way up, and go back to the house. I'll be with you in a minute or two. I have to speak to Kirk."

Ryan looked mutinous. His lower lip jutted out, then trembled. "Are you mad at me for touching the knife?"

"No. But I will be if I catch you with a sharp one in your hands again. Now go inside. You can read a book on my bed until I come."

He left, dragging his boots.

Kirk got slowly to his feet and closed the jack-knife against his thigh before slipping it into his pocket. "Don't blame the boy, Liss. It was my fault. He asked me who'd made those." He pointed to a shelf on which several carved figures stood, mostly surrealistic faces. "I told him I'd done them and he asked how I'd learned to carve things, so I explained that my dad had taught me."

Pain twisted his mouth for a moment, then he went on. "He said he didn't have a dad, so would I teach him?" He blew out a breath of air that puffed his hair back off his forehead, and followed it with a broad hand, his fingers combing roughly. "I remember what it was like, not having a dad, and I figured it wouldn't hurt."

Liss winced at the bleak expression in his eyes, and was sorry he'd been deprived of his father all through his childhood. Her major concern, however, was—had to be—her own children. "Dammit, Kirk, you don't give a four-year-old a sharp knife like that to play with."

"I didn't let him play with it! I was teaching him how to use it and I never took my eyes off him. Besides, he's nearly five."

She exhaled an angry breath. "Did he tell you he wasn't allowed to touch sharp knives?"

"Well, yes, but like I said, I wasn't letting him play with it. I was teaching him to use it safely."

"Even after you knew I preferred him not to?"

"Dammit, Liss—"

"No!" she said, stepping closer. "Dammit, *Kirk!* Those are my children, and I'm responsible for them. I make the rules and give the permission and take the heat when things go wrong, not you. I'm sick of fighting the whole damned world when it comes to the rearing of my children and I don't intend to allow any further interference on your part. Is that clear?"

He said nothing, only glared at her from his superior height. After a moment she turned and stomped angrily from the barn, leaving him standing there looking after her. She felt the ice of his gaze more intensely than she did the pellets of snow striking her burning face. She should leave. Was it worth it, staying there under the circumstances, with him and his women and his interference . . . and his kisses?

She opened the back door and stepped inside. Leaning against the door after closing it, she was aware of the warmth, the lack of drafts though the wind howled outside, and remembered the abundant food in the freezer and pantry. Oh, heavens no, she thought, she couldn't take the kids back to what they'd had. She was going to have to tough it out, and Kirk would have to learn to leave the raising of her children to her. And keep his kisses to himself.

Yet, after she'd put Ryan to bed, she couldn't help remembering the look of adoration and trust on his face as he'd looked up at Kirk and listened to his words. Boy children needed a man around. They needed a man's influence in their lives. And what Kirk had done hadn't really been so bad, had it?

Again, she'd overreacted, as she had with the dog, and the milking, and the horse. Again, she'd made a fool of herself. She crawled into bed, stacked both her pillows behind her back, and buried her nose in the novel she was reading. Several minutes passed before she realized she was turning pages but hadn't read a word. What she'd been doing was staring at the book and thinking about Kirk, remembering his scent, the feel of his mouth on hers, the strength of his embrace. It wasn't just her sons who needed a man in their lives, she needed one, too. Only . . . was Kirk Allbright, avowed bachelor, likely to be the right man?

"No," she said, dropping her book to the floor and setting her alarm clock. "Not in a million years."

"Oh, Lord . . ." Liss groaned and rolled over to shut off her alarm, then sat on the side of her bed, rocking back and forth, hugging her arms around her middle. She glanced at the window where she could hear icy bits of snow clattering as they hit. It was pitch-dark outside! This couldn't be morning! She snapped on her bedside lamp and stared at the clock to make sure she hadn't inadvertently set the alarm wrong. Nope. The dial read 5:33, and it was now up to her to prepare breakfast for a hungry rancher, who would probably want something disgusting like steak and a mound of fried potatoes topped off with half a dozen sunny-side ups. Cholesterol alley. Gahhh!

To her amazement the aroma of freshly brewed coffee greeted her as she entered the kitchen. Gratefully, she poured herself a cup and stumbled to the table. She sat there, arms folded, head resting on them, trying to wake up enough to function. She lifted her head, took a sip of coffee, then dropped her head back down after a glance at the clock showed her she wouldn't have to worry about it for another twenty minutes. After all, she couldn't start cooking until she found out what he wanted, could she?

Five

The scent and sound of frying bacon woke Liss, and she sat up to see Kirk standing in front of the stove, doing her job.

"Oh, heavens!" she said, jumping to her feet and rushing toward him. "I'm sorry. Here, let me take over. This is supposed be . . Oops, excuse me." She stumbled against his arm, joggling it as he tried to turn a slice of bacon.

"Sit down," Kirk said with a quiet laugh, putting his hands on her shoulders and holding her steady. "Look at you. You're so tired you can hardly see. Go back to bed, Liss. You're off the hook for breakfast. Any fool could see this is too early for you."

"No, no," she said.

He ignored her protest, though. Draping an arm across her shoulders, he led her back to her chair and sat her down. While she watched, still bleary-eyed, he dumped her cold coffee in the sink and poured her a fresh cup. He sat the mug in front of her, then pressed her back down when she tried to stand.

Quickly he withdrew his hand. He'd have to remember not to touch her, he thought. She was too damned tempting. Lord, look at her, all soft and creased and rumpled, her lashes tangled, her hair combed but messy, and dressed in a pair of old jeans and a hot-pink sweatshirt. She smelled deliciously of sleepy woman, soap, and toothpaste.

"Kirk, honestly," she said. "I'm awake. Let me get up. I'm supposed to be cooking breakfast. I was only . . . resting until you came in so I could ask what you wanted and—" A huge yawn interrupted her, and she rubbed her eyes before flipping her hair back from her face.

"You look about as old as Jason," he said, forcing himself to take the two long strides back to the stove before she tempted him further. He flipped the bacon out onto a paper towel to drain, then cracked three eggs into a bowl and beat them with a fork.

"Well, I'm not Jason's age," she said, getting up and dropping bread into the toaster. "I'm an adult who took on a responsibility and when I agreed to the terms of Ambrose's will, I didn't say I'd do it only if it proved to be easy or convenient. I said I'd do it, and I mean to." She met his gaze challengingly. "No arguments, Kirk."

He had to smile at her fierceness. She reminded him of a banty hen his mother once had. "All right, all right," he said placatingly. "I'm not arguing. But starting tomorrow, not today." He finished cooking the eggs, scooped them onto a plate, added several slices of bacon, then waited until she'd finished buttering the toast. "You sit down and dig into that," he ordered, shoving the plate toward her. "I'll make more."

Liss started at him and locked her hands behind her back. "I don't eat breakfast at this time of night," she said. "I eat when the kids get up, which isn't for"—she glanced at the clock again—"another two hours or more." Leaning on the counter, she eyed him balefully. "This is barbaric, you know that, don't you? It's downright uncivilized getting up to milk at this hour. Why don't you teach that cow better habits?"

He grinned as he sat down and started hungrily on his breakfast. "Cows are naturally early risers, and I like to have her needs out of the way early. This is nothing. In summer we often put in ten- or twelve- or sometimes twenty-hour days."

Liss topped up her coffee cup and filled one for him. "Twenty-hour days?"

"At calving season, yes, that can happen."

"Wow! I can see why you're so eager for Ryan to learn how to milk!"

He laughed again. "Oh, sure, I believe strongly in child labor. I expect to have him out there running the tractor for me by the time he's six, roping steer at seven." Reaching out, he brushed his fingers across the back of her hand. "I really am sorry about last night and the knife, Liss. You're right when you say he's too young for that. I'll try to be more sensible in what I teach the kids, and if I'm in doubt, I'll check with you first. Okay?"

She looked at him for a long moment, then nodded. "Okay." She chewed on her lower lip, reddening it until he wanted to lean over and stop her the best way he knew how. She prevented his acting on the impulse by saying, "I'm sorry, too, for the way I behaved. I mean, I know you weren't letting him play with the knife, and that you wouldn't have let him get hurt."

He smiled. "Thanks, Liss."

She gave him another look, then said tentatively, "Uh, Kirk? Can I ask you something? I mean, get a male point of view from you?"

He blinked. "Sure."

"Do you think I'm being overprotective?" She ran a hand through her hair, shoving it back from her face, and bit her lip again when he didn't reply. "Oh, darn, I shouldn't put you on the spot like this. Of course you think I am. My father-in-law always accuses me of that, yet my mother-in-law says I neglect the kids and expect too much of them." She sighed gustily. "How did your mother deal with raising a son all alone?"

He leaned his elbows on the table and rested his chin on his hands. "For one thing," he said, "my mom didn't have anybody undermining her authority, so she likely had it easier than you did." He shrugged. "What you see here is the finished product. How do you think she did?"

Liss had to smile. "Okay, I guess."

He swallowed a bite of toast. "I think she did okay, too, but she didn't do it all on her own, not the whole time. Tell me about your in-laws. From what Lester Brown said, I gather there have been custody questions. Why would they want to take the boys away from you?"

Liss shrugged one shoulder. "The McCalls never approved of me. Mixed blood, you see. One of my grandmothers was Japanese. And they don't approve, either," she continued, staring at her coffee mug as she turned it around and around on the table, "of a hand-to-mouth existence, even if it's a perfectly happy one filled with lots of love and laughter and togetherness." She lifted her worried gaze to him. "I'm willing to share the boys with them. I understand they're all that's left to them of their son, but I can't bear this constant threat that there'll be a messy custody battle."

"You won't have a hand-to-mouth existence here, Liss," he said soothingly.

"I know that. But while the ranch is a vast improvement over my last home, it's not exactly the luxury they think is necessary for the care and well-being of their grandchildren."

"I take it they have money? Couldn't they have helped out if they felt your kids weren't getting everything they needed?"

"Their kind of help comes with too many strings. I couldn't go on living with them, watching the boys become more and more spoiled. And since I won't live with them, they won't help."

He scooped up the last of his eggs. "How long did you live with them?"

"Quite a while. When Johnny, my husband, died, Ryan was only six months old and I was a couple of months pregnant with Jason. It seemed the sensible thing, moving in with them."

Kirk cocked one eyebrow. "But?"

"It didn't work out, so I left a year and a half ago. Ever since, they've been looking for a reason to take the kids."

He tossed the last bite of his bacon to the dog, who caught it without rising from his place in the doorway. "How did your husband die, Liss?"

Afterward Liss wondered why she told him. Maybe it was because he seemed to ask out of interest and caring, rather than curiosity.

"He committed suicide," she said. Hearing the anger and resentment in her tone, she tried to subdue it. "In a way, I guess it was my fault, mine and his parents'. Mine, for getting pregnant again, his parents for making him a spoiled, ineffectual person who couldn't deal with reality—or failure. Everything he'd ever wanted, they'd given him. Except success." And talent, she added silently. They hadn't been able to give him that, however much he wanted it.

"He was an artist, too," she went on. "We met in art school, and together we made a modest living." She didn't say that most of that living was what she earned with photography. "But then his folks . . ." She sighed. "I guess I have to say they *bought* him a one-man showing for his landscapes. He worked in oils."

Waiting for her to continue, Kirk sipped his coffee, watching her over the rim of the mug.

"And?" he prodded gently when she said no more.

She stared at the still-dark window where the snow had collected in a thick diagonal pad. A few flakes stuck higher up, then melted, running down the glass like tears. "And it bombed. And he hung himself. End of story."

Several minutes passed before Kirk stood and walked up behind her, putting his hands on her shoulders in a warm and comforting gesture. "I'm sorry, Liss."

She turned her face up to him. "I was, too. I think we would have made it, somehow. He was beginning to . . . grow up. Beginning to take responsibility. Trouble was, that time he took too much on himself. When it didn't pan out, he couldn't bear it. When I saw my in-laws trying to turn my sons into little replicas of their father by giving them everything they asked for I knew I had to get out."

He dropped his hands from her shoulders, then leaned over her to pick up his empty plate. "And now you're afraid I'll interfere," he said as he carried the plate to the sink. "I can understand that, Liss, but I promise you, I'll try not to. What I did last night was wrong, not just the knife thing, but keeping Ryan out too late. I knew you wanted him in, but I was enjoying his company. He's a nice little boy. They both are. I guess I wanted to show him something my dad showed me when I was a kid. You know, sort of pass something on to the next generation?"

She rose to pour herself more coffee, then stood by the counter looking at him. The light made his thick, straight hair gleam like polished bronze. "I thought you didn't meet your father until you were over thirty."

He retrieved his own cup, then leaned against the counter. "I'm not talking about Brose. My dad was Martin Allbright. He and my mom got married when I was eleven." He smiled sadly, looking into a distance she couldn't see. "He died eight years ago. That's when my mom told me about Brose and where to find him." He shrugged. "I'm still not sure why I came. I guess, in a way, I was hoping to find a replacement."

"Did you?"

He laughed harshly and swallowed the rest of his coffee. Setting the cup in the sink, he turned to face her. "Hell no. Brose was a hard, bitter man, and I stayed only because I needed work and he paid me well. That was when the recession was at its worst and it was damned hard to get a job in the oil fields, where I'd worked since I was eighteen. Also, I found I liked the life. After I'd been here a couple of years, he said he might leave me the ranch if I worked hard enough for it. I'm still not sure why."

"You were his son, Kirk, though he didn't know about you until you were an adult. It must have counted for something."

He shook his head. "Not a lot, because I'm also Betty Allbright's son, and believe me, his bitterness toward her for not telling him about me years ago knew no bounds."

They were silent for a minute, then Liss said softly, "In the letter he left me, he said that his soul died when my aunt did, and that he only got it back when Reverend Daisy showed him the way."

Again, Kirk's laugh held little humor. "Reverend Daisy," he said, "scared the devil out of him. Literally. He met her after he was diagnosed with cancer, and any man when faced with death, even a man like Brose, is up for grabs if the right preacher comes along."

"So," Liss said, "because she got him and turned him around, Mrs. Healey and I get to share your inheritance, because Uncle Ambrose wanted to make amends for his wrongdoings, real or imaginary. Doesn't the injustice of that bother you?"

He gazed thoughtfully across the room for several moments. "No. Mrs. Healey worked like a slave for him, and your aunt, if she'd lived, might have asked you here herself." Before she could move away, he stepped closer to her and slid a hand around the back of her neck. "Besides, I think having you here is going to have its . . . rewards."

Mama cat purred contentedly to her mewing babies. The kitchen was warm and redolent of bacon and coffee, creating an aura of security that Liss found oddly disturbing. She wasn't sure she wanted to feel safe and warm and protected here, wasn't certain if it was wise to let Kirk look to her for rewards. Even as she fought it, a heavy heat curled deep inside her, making her shift restlessly. As if it had been a signal, Kirk bent down and took her mouth in a long, leisurely kiss that made her tremble from the inside out.

"I want to do a lot of that," he murmured moments later, sliding his lips over her cheek, then nibbling on her earlobe. "Every time I look at you, that's what I want to do."

"Kirk, please," she whispered, gazing at him, feeling bemused, weak, and dazed.

His breath was warm on her face, his eyes hooded as he smiled at her. "Please what?" He traced the shape of one cheekbone with a thumb, then grazed over the scar on her chin. "Kiss you again? I plan to. But I have to catch my breath first."

Heat pulsed through her as she let herself think about kissing him again. After a moment, while her imagination leaped as wildly as her pulse, she shook her head. "No." She shivered and inched back from him, wrapping her arms around her middle. "Don't do it again." Even to herself, though, she sounded tentative and unsure.

He stood back and looked at her for several seconds, then nodded. "Whatever you say." His tone held amusement. "Unless you mean not ever?" He tilted his head to one side, clearly awaiting a reply.

"No!" She shook her head vigorously. "Uh, I mean, yes. I . . . Dammit, I don't know what I mean." She took another step away, resentful that he could create this kind of turmoil within her, with need and fear and yearning all mixed up together, and appear so unaffected himself. It simply pointed up the differences between them— he with his obvious experience and she with her relative lack of it. "I think we should stick with being friends," she finished.

"Okay, Liss. I'd like to have you as a friend."

She flicked a glance at him, saw the laughter in his eyes, the warmth, the caring, and ached to respond to it. After all, friendship didn't have to preclude . . . other things, did it? It would be so very easy to close the distance between them, to reach for him and feel his arms fold around her again. . . .

Abruptly, as if the subject weren't worth pursuing, he shrugged and said, "I have a bunch of hungry cattle waiting for their morning feed, so I suppose I'd better get at it."

She nodded and watched silently as he tugged on his heavy jacket, his gloves and planted his Stetson square on his head. As he opened the back door, she saw that it was still dark. He strode outside without a backward glance, and she sat at the table, head in her hands, wondering if her world would ever stand true on its axis again. This was unbelievable! Here she was, on her first real working day at Whittier Ranch, and she'd not only blown her morning task by sitting idly by and watching Kirk cook his own breakfast, she had told him things she rarely told anybody. She had listened to confidences she suspected he didn't often share. She had let him kiss her until she couldn't see straight—and it wasn't even daylight!

To Liss's relief Kirk poked his head in the door briefly at midmorning and said not to expect him for lunch. That gave her more time to get herself under control before having to face him again. When the boys woke up from their afternoon nap, it had stopped snowing and the sun shone brightly again. She dressed them and herself warmly, stuffed film, filters, and lenses into her smallest tote, and draped a camera around her neck. It was time she investigated this ranch Uncle Ambrose had made her part of.

She stepped out onto the back porch, then halted at the sight of Kirk. He was in the yard with his dog, busy embellishing their snowman by sculpting arms across its chest. Under one of those arms he'd stuck a battered stable broom, and on the snowman's head perched an old slouch hat. Kirk looked up as Ryan and Jason shouted to him, then grinned self-consciously and tilted his Stetson back.

"Hi, buddy," he said to Ryan as the little boy raced to his side. Kirk's eyes, though, silver-gray and full of blatant appreciation, were on Liss. Her emotions caromed around inside her, emotions she wasn't sure she liked, but his smile affected her as it always did with a delicious quivering in her stomach.

Jason tore his hand from her too-tight grip and ran to Kirk's side as well. Liss, however, remained frozen on the porch, mesmerized by his intent gaze, her hands suddenly unsteady on her camera as her heart and stomach temporarily traded places, then flip-flopped back. She forced herself to ignore those sensations and tear her gaze free, then slipped off her gloves to take several shots out across the backyard. When she finished and ran down the back steps, she slipped as she hit the snow. Kirk shot out a steadying hand to catch her, and she had to swallow a time or two before she could even say hello.

He gestured toward her camera. "Back at work, I see."

This, she could talk about, Liss thought happily. "I hope so. I don't have a lot of experience with the effects snow has on light, shadow and contrast, but my agent wants me to experiment."

Kirk heard the lilt of excitement and enthusiasm in her tone. "Agent?"

She nodded, and explained how she'd taken the time on the trip up to the ranch to get some work done and sent it to an old friend who had acted as her agent before. "I talked to him again this morning and he's as excited as I am about the opportunities I'll have up here for some really great stuff." With a small shrug, she added, "But he's also an old friend, so the proof of my work will naturally be in the selling."

Kirk stiffened. Her agent was a man, and an old friend? How good a friend? The question stirred up something primitive and shockingly possessive in him that he didn't like at all.

Liss misinterpreted his sharp glance, and her mouth pulled taut. "Don't worry," she said. "I won't neglect my household duties. You'll still get fed, even if I do take an hour off now and then to exercise my camera."

"I'm not worried about that." Kirk rescued the broom from Ryan's energetic attempts to brush snow off it, then followed as Liss ran after Jason. He'd decided to explore and was heading straight for the fenced pasture where the horse cavorted. The dog beat her to it, not touching the little boy, but herding him back toward her.

"Hold it, bub!" she said, swinging Jason up onto her hip as Kirk, with Ryan in tow, sauntered up. "Remember, I said we'd stick together until we know what's safe and what's not." She set him down in a tractor rut and turned him loose with the dog.

"How about I take you on a guided tour," Kirk said. "It's a good idea for all three of you to know where you shouldn't go for your own safety."

Liss hesitated, then asked, "Don't you have work to do? I'd hate to keep you from important things."

Kirk was astounded to realize she was serious. In his experience, women were all too happy to keep a man from his work. They saw it as a rival for his attention and went out of their way to draw him from it.

"I hate to admit it, Liss," he said, walking alongside her as she followed her sons, "but this time of year, there isn't a lot to do on a ranch of this size except keeping the animals fed and the equipment in running order. Besides, what could be more important than showing my partner over our spread?" He smiled and took her gloved hand in his.

Partner, Liss thought, casting a sidelong glance at him. The word had a nice sound. It was a long time since she'd felt like anybody's partner. And even longer since she'd walked anywhere with her hand held in such a strong clasp, with a warmth she could feel right through to her soul.

Twisting her hand loose from that all-too-comfortable clasp, she ran a few paces ahead, then turned and walked backward up a gentle slope, her camera in constant action.

When Kirk realized Jason was having trouble in the deep snow, he dropped his big hat onto Ryan's head and lifted Jason onto his shoulders. Ryan beamed up at him from under the hat, then grabbed on to Marsh's collar as Kirk suggested, letting the strong dog pull him up the hill. From his high perch Jason squealed with delight as he clutched Kirk's forehead with both hands and bounced on his shoulders. Liss's heart filled with happiness as she saw how much fun her children were having, how relaxed and at home they were after only three days there. Three days? Yes. She remembered with shock how relaxed and at home she'd felt that morning in Kirk's arms. Exactly the way she'd felt Friday night, and Sunday . . .

Darn it, she thought, she had to stop what was happening to her. It was fine for her children to succumb to his charms, fine for them to adapt so easily to living on the ranch with him, but it wasn't fine for her. She was an adult, a supposedly intelligent one, and intelligent adults didn't leap into situations simply because it felt good. They acted with caution, prudently and thoughtfully, she told herself severely, and didn't simply let circumstances carry them along like a piece of wood in a fast-moving river.

Satisfied with her little lecture, Liss panned her camera around and found the barn and the horse in her viewfinder. She turned the lens for better focus, and as she caught the prancing animal in mid-leap, a laugh burst forth spontaneously.

"What's funny?" Kirk asked.

She turned and focused on his face, adjusting the lens, bringing him closer, closer, close enough to see the slight stubble of his beard, the question in his eyes, the amusement. She'd meant merely to look at him for a moment, but she was captivated by the expression in his eyes. The stark shadow from Jason's arm bisected his face, contrasting with the bright arc of sunlight that slanted over his left cheek, turning his skin ruddy and his blond hair to molten gold. His neck rose in a strong column from the loose collar of his jacket, bracketed by Jason's stubby legs, and his hands looked enormous wrapped around the child's ankles.

Another slight adjustment of her telephoto lens brought his image close enough to kiss.

Quickly she dropped the camera. "Your horse looks as if he belongs on a carousel," she said.

As he turned to gaze down the hill toward the barn, she captured his strong profile. Click and whir . . . click and whir . . . She danced several feet to one side, seeking a different angle. Kirk's eyes followed her. He turned to face the lens no matter where she went. She continued to click and click and click, until she realized what she was doing. Finally lowering the camera, she lowered her gaze, too, and fumbled to change films. Angling higher this time, she captured several shots of Jason's laughing face with the bright blue sky behind him, and a couple of Ryan, who tended to hide from the camera. He was visible only as a huge hat covering most of his face above his grin, and his hands were buried in Marsh's thick nape fur.

Kirk set Jason down and the two boys tumbled to the snow, flattening out and making angels while the dog jumped around them, licking faces, eliciting giggles and shrieks. To Liss's shock, a rush of tears flooded her eyes as she watched. Before she could blink them away, they spilled over, hot on her cold cheeks. With a frown and a muttered curse, Kirk leaped toward her.

"What's wrong?" he asked, grasping her hand and wiping away the tears himself.

She swallowed hard, shook her head, and sniffled. "I don't know. Nothing. I just . . . Look at them. They're so happy!"

He relaxed, then nodded, smiling down at her. Lifting her hand again, he stroked her face from her temple to her chin. "And how about their mom?"

Slowly, she smiled. "I think I am, too."

"Good." His tone was filled with satisfaction. "I think the country agrees with you, city girl."

"Don't be silly," she said, laughing. "How could a place without so much as a regular daily paper agree with me?"

"Maybe there are . . . compensations."

"Maybe," she said breathlessly, and to show him

what she meant, she aimed her camera at the mountain peaks gleaming in the sun. She told herself that that was what she meant, that she was happy merely because her children were. That was what made being there worthwhile, the snow and cold and Mrs. Healey and the lack of a regular daily paper notwithstanding.

It had nothing to do with Kirk Allbright's smile. Nothing at all.

"This is how I feed the stock," Kirk said, putting Jason down again now that they could walk in the tractor's ruts along a fence line beside long rows of feeding racks. "See that haystack over there?" He pointed to a snow-covered mound. Several more like it dotted the landscape near other pastures. "There's fodder under a tarp there, and every morning, more often when the weather's bad, I come out with the tractor and haul bales of hay close to the fence line, then heave them into the bins."

He glanced at Liss and smiled. "That's what I was doing the day you arrived—what I'd been doing for several days prior to that."

She bit her lip. "And there I was, screaming at you for not being home to let me in. No wonder you weren't happy to see me."

He touched her face with one warm finger. She wondered how it could be so warm in the thin, cold mountain air. Between series of photographs, she was quick to put her gloves back on. "It didn't take me long to change my mind," he said, dropping his hand to her shoulder. "One taste of your . . . chocolate cake and I was done for." His words said "cake" while his eyes said "kisses."

Liss shifted sideways to escape the warm weight

of that hand. "Duncan Hines had more to do with that cake than I did," she said, feeling inordinately hurt by his words, regardless of what his eyes might say. Yet, she asked herself, was there anything wrong with being appreciated for baking cakes? Cakes and kisses. Food and sex. Those were important ingredients in a man's happiness, weren't they? He claimed to have provided food for himself quite efficiently since his father died, though he was happy to turn the kitchen over to her. As for sex . . . It seemed he hadn't been lacking anything in that department either, so why was he flirting with her? Simply because, like her cooking, he thought her body might be available? Since it was conveniently here, he might as well put it to use?

Not wanting him to see the confusion in her eyes, she backed away into the deep snow that had drifted against a nearby fence. She floundered as she tried to get a long shot of the line of feeding stands with the cattle busily eating, and the dog circling the man and boys, keeping them together in a small herd. She needed more altitude, and decided to climb the fence. She hooked her heels on the strands of barbed wire and held on to a post. Spotting her, Marsh barked and raced over to her, catching the toe of her boot in his teeth.

She screamed and nearly toppled over onto the other side of the fence, but Kirk snatched her down unceremoniously, tumbling to the snow with her.

"For the love of Mike, woman," he said impatiently, "what are you doing?"

"Your dog tried bite off my foot!"

"He did not." He stood and hauled her up. "Marsh was simply doing what he does best," he went on, brushing snow off her. "Trying to keep his people together. You should be grateful. You damn near fell into the pasture with the bulls."

She glanced over her shoulder. "Bulls? I thought they were more cows."

He sighed gustily and shook his head. "Look again. Those are bulls, city girl, big, bad, mean bulls that can run at the speed of a freight train and hit with the impact of a locomotive."

She looked again, frowning. "What's the difference?"

He laughed and swung an arm around her shoulders, bringing her up close against his side. "Are you trying to tell me you don't know the difference between males and females? I'd be more than happy to offer a few anatomy lessons."

Liss felt heat rise in her cheeks as she stepped away from him. "I know the difference, of course. Basically. But at forty paces, cattle are cattle."

He shook his head. "Check the shapes, photographer, the lines and angles. Bulls and men are pretty much the same. At forty paces you can tell the difference between a man and a woman, can't you?" He didn't wait for a reply. "Broader shoulders," he said, taking her hands and lifting them to his shoulders, making her very aware of the breadth of them under his sheepskin jacket, "and narrower hips." Instead of moving her hands down to his hips, he cradled hers in his warm grip, smoothing his palms over her jeans, pulling her toward him. "Bulls and men are hard. Women are soft," he added, bending to brush his mouth over hers.

"Hey," she said, half laughing as she slipped out of his loose clasp. "I told you I don't need anatomy lessons. Now that you've pointed it out, I can see the difference in shape between cows and bulls."

His eyes held a devilish light. "And men and women? Or should we explore that one further?"

"No," she said. "We shouldn't. I know all I need to know."

"But," he murmured, touching her cheek again, "I don't. And I'd like—very much—to explore them with you."

"Let's explore the ranch instead . . . partner."

He gave her a crooked smile and sighed. "Sure . . . partner." He took her hand and, together with the children and the dog, they set off again.

"You really love this place, don't you?" Liss asked some time later.

Kirk smiled. "Yeah, I do. There's something about the land, the animals, the good growing things, even the elements I have to fight to keep it all together. It's a challenge I could never leave."

Liss thought about Gina saying that she hadn't truly been trying to lure him away, that she could live here year-round. Had that been the argument between them, the one for which Gina wanted forgiveness?

Kirk leaned on a fence post, gazing around the pasture where they stood, and smiled. "Even at forty below, breaking ice so the cows can drink, or heaving fodder until my back breaks, or cutting hay in the heat with chaff itching in . . . strange places, I wouldn't trade it, as precarious as it is."

"Precarious?"

He turned to face her. "It doesn't take much to wipe out a rancher. Loss of stock to disease, machinery going belly-up, drought—which means no hay for winter feed, which means you have to buy it. Lots of things can hurt. Some can kill."

Liss was thoughtful for several moments. "Like having four extra people to support, two more wages to pay?" She suspected he had been managing the books all right without Mrs. Healey's help, and if he had a wife, he wouldn't have to pay her the dividend he paid Liss, right out of the ranch's profits.

He smiled again and touched her face with his cold fingers. "Don't you worry about that. The ranch can support all of us."

But Liss couldn't help wondering if finances hadn't had a lot to do with Kirk's initial resentment of the way Ambrose had arranged things. It wasn't, when she thought about it, very fair to him at all.

Six

The afternoon sped by, and Liss knew they must have covered miles of territory yet seen very little of the ranch. When they returned to the house, she leaned against the pasture fence admiring Kirk's frisky, black-maned horse, Chieftain, who spent only nights and very bad days in his stable in the smaller barn.

"You could learn to ride," Kirk said, leaning beside her, his shoulder large and warm, his bulk blocking the cold wind. He tipped his hat back as he swept his gaze over her. "You have an inborn grace that would make you a natural."

"I was thinking the same thing," she said. "That I should learn, that is. I could really get out there with my camera, then, couldn't I?" She swept her arm in an arc. "And with the kids so enthusiastic about getting ponies in the spring, I guess I'll have to try it again, if only to stay with them and make sure they don't stray into bull territory."

Kirk grinned. "Now that you know the difference."

She met his gaze. "And the danger."

He sobered and she read the question—and the intent—in his eyes. Her heart pounded hard as she acknowledged that there were other, greater dangers on this ranch, and that Kirk meant to lead her into them if she offered him the least bit of encouragement. She did not. There was more to her, more to life, than chocolate cake.

Ryan's plaintive "Can we go in now, Mom? My legs are tired of walking" broke the taut silence between them.

"Okay," she said, reluctantly fitting the lens cap on her camera. The scenery kept calling her to crest one more hill, round one more corner, take one more photograph. The light was failing, though, and there'd be little more photography that day. "Let's go. You can watch cartoons while I get dinner ready."

The boys, in spite of their tired legs, ran on ahead, laughing and shouting as they jockeyed for position going up the back steps. The sound of the door slamming behind them rang in the clear, cold air. Liss gave in to temptation and quickly fitted her telephoto lens onto the camera for a couple of last long shots out over the silvery river and the Cariboo range to the west, where an iridescent mother-of-pearl sunset created a backdrop for the starkly black mountain crests.

"For a lady so reluctant to come and live in the 'wilderness,'" Kirk said when she was done, "you seem to have taken to it very nicely today." He took her bag and draped it over his shoulder.

She smiled up at him as they walked along the tractor ruts toward the house. "I've enjoyed myself this afternoon. This is a very beautiful part of the world."

"Yes, it is, and you'll have plenty of opportunity to ply your trade, so you can afford to take a break when the sun sets." He took her hand again. "Winter lasts a long time up here in the mountains."

Her entire body responded to the feel of his rough, hard fingers wrapping around hers, then leaped to full attention as he drew her to a halt at the corner of the garage. He touched her chin with one finger, brushing it over the scar that seemed to fascinate him. His thumbnail traced its shape, then smoothed over her lower lip, making her wonder if he was about to kiss her again, making her wish he would. She turned her face away. Dammit, she shouldn't want his touch so much! She shouldn't let him make her go weak in the legs and even weaker in the head. She shook herself free and continued on toward the house. He walked along beside her, but then stopped her at the bottom of the steps.

"Don't go in yet," he said, gently grasping her arm. "Let's watch the sunset fade."

She turned toward the west, then glanced at him. "You're not looking at the sunset."

"I can see it reflected in your eyes. You have beautiful eyes," he whispered. "Soft and brown one minute, then bright and shiny, almost black, another. They speak of your moods." His thumb stroked her lower lip, leaving a burning, tingling sensation in its wake.

She could scarcely talk. "Kirk, don't . . ."

"Don't what?"

"Don't touch me like that."

Again, his voice was low, intimate. "Why not?"

"Because—because you're only doing it because I'm . . . handy. Let's face it, you sure don't need me. You have plenty of women in your life as it is."

He dropped his hands, and his eyes glinted

silver in the fading light. "And what 'women' might those be?" he asked in a dangerously soft tone.

She raised her chin determinedly. "Gina, for one."

"Gina's a . . . " He grinned sourly. "Do I dare say it? A thing of the past."

"Is she?"

Kirk sighed inwardly as he watched doubt and perplexity play across Liss's face. He wanted, suddenly and almost irresistibly, to kiss her deeply, for a long time, until those doubts were erased. Unable to stop himself, he slid a hand into her thick hair and bent closer . . . then hesitated. Hell, what was he doing? His future was all mapped out, and it didn't include a permanent, full-time woman, which was all this woman would ever want from a man. Dammit, it was what she had every right to expect! What she deserved. He knew that, so what the hell was he doing tempting fate this way? Tempting himself!

"And Kristy?" she asked quickly, twisting free.

He scowled. He didn't want her to leave yet. He wanted to have at least the subject of other women out of the way, so it wouldn't crop up between them again. Pulling her back around, he slid his hands under her red ski jacket and locked them at the small of her back.

"I met Kristy two years ago when I sprained an ankle. She works in the local hospital as an X-ray technician. We dated a few times after that, then stopped seeing each other that way. We're friends. She's dating a truck driver now."

He wondered what Liss would do if he pulled her more tightly against him, letting her know beyond any doubt that she was the woman who interested him, moved him, made him ache. He resisted the urge. It would be too hard to control, and something told him that with this woman and the potent effect she had on him, control was absolutely necessary until he knew exactly where this wild attraction was headed.

"And Patty?" she asked, breaking into his thoughts.

He was so astounded, he relaxed his hold on her. "Patty? What about her?"

"Isn't she another of your girlfriends, ex- or otherwise?"

Liss clenched her teeth as his laughter rang out. She resented his laughing at her, but his next words proved the laughter was not at her expense.

"Not by any stretch of anybody's imagination, except for hers, when she was seventeen and developed a crush on me when I first came here. She drove me nuts for three months, following me around. But she grew up and got over it, thank heavens. Now she drives me crazy in a different way, playing the vamp to help me convince her cousin Gina that it's all over between us, and that if I want anything from her it's friendship."

He sobered and scowled. "As you saw, though, Gina's not prepared to accept that, so friendship's out, I guess. No matter. I can do without her brand."

His expression, a blend of masculine confusion, concern, and embarrassment, did more to convince Liss than any of his words had, and all at once she felt lighthearted and carefree. "Friendship's a fine thing to have," she said, adroitly slipping out of his loose embrace. "I recommend it highly." She grinned at him over her shoulder as she ran up the steps.

"Are you going to be busy this morning?" Kirk asked as he came in for breakfast on Wednesday,

Marsh at his heels. The dog lay down on his blanket in the utility room, while Kirk, after knocking the snow off his boots, continued on into the kitchen, carrying two large bottles of milk.

Liss set her crossword book aside and looked up with a smile that faltered as her pulse went mad. Dammit, when was she going to get used to seeing him come in, watching him tip that Stetson of his to the back of his head, smiling at her from under his thick fall of fair hair? When was she going to stop responding? Next thing you know, she told herself, he'd tip his hat back and she'd start drooling like Pavlov's dogs.

"I've enrolled the boys in preschool," she said, jumping quickly to her feet to put his breakfast on the table. When he came in from milking, he came in starved. It took an enormous amount of food to keep him filled up.

"This will be their first day," she went on, setting a pan of hot biscuits on the table. "All I have to do is take them there and drop them off. Why, was there something you wanted me to do?"

She opened the refrigerator to put the fresh milk inside, and he leaned over her as he set his hat up on top. She drew in a deep breath of his outdoors scent, then quickly slipped away to fetch the rest of his breakfast from the oven.

"You said your furniture is arriving tomorrow," he said as he sat down at the table, "so I thought if I'm going to get a carpet laid in the playroom, it would be easier to do it before there's much stuff in there. How about I go with you to take the boys to school, and while they're occupied, we'll buy the carpet?"

"Sure," she said. "But can you expect to find a carpet layer who'll come on only a few hours' notice?"

He laughed as he spread butter on a biscuit, then popped half of it into his mouth at once. He tapped his chest with one finger as he swallowed. "I'm the carpet layer, city girl. Out here, we do things for ourselves."

"You know how to lay carpet?"

He shrugged. "I've never done it before, but I've read up on it." He didn't add that he'd been reading up on it the past couple of nights because, tired as he was from a long day of work, something—or someone—tended to keep him awake. So he read.

Liss laughed softly. "Carpet laying by the book. This," she murmured, "I've gotta see."

He grinned. "O ye of little faith . . ."

"What are those things for?" Jason asked. He tried to grab one of the narrow strips of wood, studded with tiny, sharp nails, that Kirk had set on the floor immediately after they arrived back home.

"Whoa!" Kirk lunged in time to prevent Jason's hands from being lacerated. "Don't touch! Those are called tack strips and they're very sharp. They'd hurt you if you picked them up. I'm going to nail them along the floor like this, right up close to the wall, with the pointed parts up. When I put the carpet down, it gets hooked on the little nails and stays where I put it."

He had talked too long for Jason's short attention span. The three-year-old had darted away before he was finished, and launched himself onto the roll of green rubber underlay. He mounted it as if it were a horse and bounced violently on it, shouting "Giddyap!" repeatedly and with increasing volume.

"Neat," Ryan said, kneeling beside Kirk to peer at the tack strips, but not touching. "Can I help?" He picked up Kirk's tape measure, pushed the button, and laughed wildly as nine feet of steel tape snaked back inside its casing with a wicked *whish!* Startled when the end whipped past his nose, Kirk jumped and knocked over a can of nails. They tinkled and rolled and spread over a great area.

"Sorry, guys, it's nap time," Liss said, seeing a crazed, trapped look enter Kirk's eyes. "Let's go."

The boys protested, but she got them settled in their beds. Within moments both were asleep, worn out from their morning at preschool. Liss smiled, remembering Jason's expression earlier that morning when he'd realized she was leaving him at the school. He'd looked as though she were abandoning him in a leaky boat in shark-infested waters with a storm coming up. By the time she and Kirk returned two hours later to collect them, though, neither of the boys wanted to leave. They were hoping to stay for three hours tomorrow.

Back downstairs, she reentered the playroom. "Now," she said, shoving her sleeves up. "Tell me what I can do to help." This was the way to do things, she thought. Keep it businesslike. Nothing more than two partners working together on a project of mutual interest.

Kirk looked up from his task of fastening the last of the tack strips to the floor. "Believe me, you've already helped. Sometimes, too many hands make more work, especially when some of those hands belong to little guys."

"Do you think I don't know that? Why do you think mothers invented naps?"

His eyes danced. "I can see that naps are a real boon."

He grunted as he heaved the roll of wafflelike

underlay over to one wall. "Stand on the end of this, will you, while I get the rest of it spread out."

She did as he asked, but as he unrolled the bulky stuff, her weight wasn't enough to keep the entire end down. The two corners rolled back up and curled around her knees, then her waist, creeping toward her shoulders as Kirk got farther away.

"Uh, what did the book say about this?" she asked as she fought to hold the underlay back.

Kirk turned from his task and gaped at her. "It . . . didn't," he said. "Hmm. Well, hold it down as best you can."

She spread her feet apart, but that helped only minimally. She bent forward at the waist, putting her hands on the floor, too, and managed to hold down a larger area, but the awkward position was not one she could maintain for long. Spying a hammer in the doorway, she walked her hands forward and managed to grab it. With a grunt, she started back the way she'd come, inchworm-style. When Kirk burst into laughter, she glanced at him upside down between her knees.

"What are you doing?" he asked, kneeling on the floor and staring at her over his shoulder. "You look as if you're playing Twister!"

"Getting . . . this," she said. She paused long enough to show him the hammer, then walked her hands back toward her feet while circling her feet around so she faced one corner. She tossed the hammer into the corner, and its weight held the underlay down—at least at that one spot. Then she collapsed onto her stomach, and found she could cover a much greater portion of the end by lying flat and stretching her arms as high as she could over her head. Wriggling, she positioned herself so that most of the edge lay flat under her, then gave

Kirk a triumphant grin. "There," she said. "That's got it under control."

He was still staring at her. "I think the author of that how-to book missed a bet."

"Me, too. This is really quite comfortable. You were right to get the thickest, most expensive brand. Let me know when you're ready for step two." She closed her eyes.

Kirk's mouth went dry as he gazed at her. Maybe the carpet pad was under control, but he sure wasn't. The sight of her cute bottom sticking up in the air as she walked around on her hands and feet, her hair dangling down like a silky black mop, had set up the kind of reaction in him that he was fast beginning to associate with her. Now, seeing her lying there with her eyes shut and that perky grin on her face, her hair still tumbled all around, her breasts plumped against the floor, her backside in delicious profile in her tight jeans, he had to force himself to get back to work.

"Well, damn," he said as he wrestled with the rest of the recalcitrant stuff. When he arrived at the far end of the room, he discovered he had the same problem she'd had. As long as he stood on it, the pad stayed still—in that spot. The moment he moved to try to reach something with which to hold it down, it sneaked up behind him and flopped over his back. If he turned and flattened that section of it, the other corner curled over him. After a few minutes of futile fight, he, too, lay down. He faced Liss across the length of the floor and laughed at her startled expression.

"Why not?" he said, resting his head on the heel of one hand. "You're right. This seems to work. If we stay here a couple of weeks, the damn thing might behave. You game?" He dropped his head down and closed his eyes. "How do mothers feel about naps for big boys?"

Liss giggled and hoped Mrs. Healey wouldn't come in and catch them lying on the floor like idiots. She'd tell Lester Brown on both of them. "Why don't we hook it on the little nails?" she asked, turning from him long enough to cast a wary glance at the line of tack strip behind her.

"Because it would tear. Besides, the book said it had to be cut an inch shorter than the carpet on purpose, so it won't reach the strips. Nope, it seems to me we're stuck here. If either of us tries to stand, it's going to roll up on us again. I only wish we were a little closer together. It seems a shame to waste an opportunity like this." He patted the rubber. "You're right. It is comfortable. Why don't you slide on over here and we'll get comfortable together?" His smile was full of teasing—at least her mind thought he was teasing. Her body, on the other hand, had a different idea. Her body wanted to take him seriously.

"Come on," he urged, patting the floor beside him again. "You have one of your corners pinned down, so it'll be less trouble for you to move than for me."

She thought of all the trouble she could get into if she did as he asked. "I thought we were going to simply be friends."

His eyes widened. "You think I'm being un-friendly?"

She shook her head, captivated by the power of his gaze, even though he was at least fourteen feet away. "No. I think maybe you're being too friendly. I feel . . . safer with this much space between us."

He cocked an eyebrow. "And safer is better?"

"I think so."

"What if I were to prove something different to you?"

She laughed, feeling quite secure where she was—as long as he stayed where he was. "I don't see how you can. As you said, it looks as if we're stuck here."

"Oh, I don't know." He rolled toward her experimentally. The underlay curled along behind him like a big green comber on a Hawaiian shore.

He turned over a second time, a third, a fourth, and then was gone, lost in the rolls of rubber. Liss laughed helplessly as he flailed exaggeratedly and beat at the stuff, shoving it off only to have it flop back down and cover him again. "Help," he said, poking his head out. He was halfway across the room by now. "I'm being swallowed!"

"Stay right where you are." She gingerly got to her feet and walked toward the doorway. The sticky rubber followed her, all but the corner that was pinned and the center where Kirk lay wrapped. "I'll go and get some heavy things to put on the ends. Don't move, or we'll have to start all over again."

She was back in minutes, to find him where she had left him, holding one arm erect to protect himself from the loose corner she'd left, the other fending off the rest of the roll. Pushing the corner flap ahead of her with one hand and taking long strides, Liss flattened the pad out before her. Once it lay properly again, she set a can of pumpkin on it, then followed along toward the hammer, setting down other heavy cans as she went.

"Okay," she said, "while I get some more cans, you roll back to your end and I'll get it pinned down, too."

Instead, he snaked out a hand and caught her ankle, stopping her in her tracks. "Hey," he said. "I was heading over here for a reason, remember? You go back there and lie down again and wait for me."

She stared down at his hand. It was so large, it wrapped easily around her ankle. Slowly, he slid it up her calf as far as he could push the leg of her jeans. All the while his smoldering gaze was on her face, watching her reaction. "You have silky skin to go with your silky hair," he said softly. "Come on down here with me. Lie beside me and we'll roll over a time or two and no will ever know we're in here. I bet you're never been kissed inside a roll of carpet underlay."

Liss tried to be serious and failed utterly. The picture his words painted was too ridiculous. She laughed. "That's a bet you'd win."

"Then why not try it?" He sat up quickly, thrusting aside the floppy rubber, and clasped her hand. He tugged until she fell half on top of him, half on top of the roll. "You might like it. Friends do things like this, you know."

She shook her head and tried to scramble away, but the waffle texture caught at her socks and her knees and her elbows, while Kirk caught her around the waist, holding her easily. Still laughing, she subsided as the underlay flopped over them several times, then settled down, cocooning them in a private, green-tinged world.

He touched the scar on her chin as he gazed at her with sleepy, hooded eyes, his mouth only centimeters from hers and curved into a smile that snatched her breath away.

Slowly she lifted a hand and curved it around his jaw, discovering hard, strong bones under her skin and the short stubble of his beard. Excitement skittered along her nerves as he clenched his teeth and drew in a sharp breath, obviously affected by her touch.

"I've never had a friend like you before," she said, her voice tremulous and throaty as she wavered on the brink of laughter.

"And I'm feeling very . . . friendly, Liss." His voice was husky and his breath brushed her cheek when he drew her even closer. "I was attracted to you the first time I saw you standing in front of your house, with your hair all wind tossed and your skirt blown tight against your backside and those ridiculous, high-heeled city-girl shoes making your legs look like a million dollars." He ran one hand down over her hip, defining the shape of her thigh. "And then you arrived here, and it got stronger. It hasn't quit any since. Kiss me."

She didn't say no.

His first kiss was a mere brushing of his lips over hers. Even that tentative skimming touch sent her pulse rate into overdrive, and she shivered. He closed his eyes and kissed her again, and this time she placed a hand on the back of his head, holding him to her. She parted her lips for him, admitting his tongue and meeting it with her own. When he drew back, her vision was blurred, but not so far gone that she couldn't see the bemused, questioning gaze he turned on her.

A smile curved his chiseled mouth. "You were right to recommend friendship. I really like your style."

"I . . . like yours, too," she whispered, and suddenly what had started as a lighthearted game became deadly serious. Her heart pounded hard in her chest as Kirk's smile faded and his eyes grew dark with desire. She clenched her hands in his shirtfront, trembling against him as he took her mouth in a deep, searching kiss. He must have found what he was looking for, because he made a soft, pleased sound in his throat. Tangling his hand in her hair, he tilted her head back and kissed her scar again, then her throat, her ears, her eyelids, before returning to her mouth.

Liss tingled all over—from her palms, spread across his chest; to her legs, tangled with his; to her belly, where his hard arousal pressed.

Even when the kisses stopped and they lay there enveloped in their small, secret world, breathing raggedly as they gazed into each other's eyes, it took her several moments to be able to whisper, "Was this in your how-to book?"

"There are no instruction books for what's happening," he said hoarsely. "You send me right out of control."

His words, the expression in his eyes, the tone of his voice, frightened her more than anything ever had in her entire life. Her heart raced. Her breathing grew labored. She put her hand on his chin and held him away. She didn't like the idea of his being out of control, not when she was so close to being the same.

"No, stop," she said. "Let's stick with being friends. The usual kind. Don't, please," she added when he tried to kiss her again. "Don't play your seduction games with me! I've been out of circulation a long time. I don't know the rules anymore." Moreover, she'd never learned any rules that could help her with a man like this, one who showed and said so positively what he wanted, what he expected of her. One who would, and did, demand equal participation.

He drew her hand to his lips and kissed her palm, then held it against his chest. "This is no seduction game, Liss," he said tautly. "This is basic man-woman stuff and the rules haven't changed any. You know them as well as I do, but if you want them spelled out for you, I'll oblige. What we have here is more than a simple attraction I can walk away from. I don't merely want a few kisses and some laughs. I want you."

Again, he'd shocked her by being blunt. This time, though, she refused to retreat. "No," she said firmly.

"No, what?" he asked quietly. "I haven't asked for anything." He paused. "Yet."

Liss shook her head to clear the dizziness, then reached up both arms to push the underlay back, giving her more light and air. The dizzy sensation remained. He *hadn't* asked anything. He'd simply made a statement. He wanted her. His steady gaze had told her it was true even before he'd said the words. She tried to shift her body away from his, away from the other, more potent evidence.

"That doesn't mean we can't be friends, though," he said. "It means we have a much more important reason for being friends."

"Don't," she said, then cleared her throat and added with greater conviction. "Don't want me, Kirk. I didn't come here looking for anything like this."

He helped her hold the floppy rubber stuff back, his gaze never leaving her face. "I know that. I wasn't expecting it either, but now that it's happening, why should we deny it?"

She wondered what he'd say if he knew that nothing remotely like this had happened to her before, that no man, not even her husband, had had the power to turn her to molten liquid inside the way he did. She wondered if he could tell that she wanted him just as much as he obviously wanted her. His eyes were dark, unreadable, and she had no idea what he was thinking, but then she stopped trying to figure it out because he was kissing her again with her full cooperation as the underlay enveloped them once more.

Minutes later, she said, gasping for breath, "I don't think friends should do things like this to each other."

"Of course they should," he said, his voice a low growl. "When they want each other the way we do." And Lord, did he want her! Kirk thought. He wanted her now. He wanted her bad. He wanted her close. He slid his hand from her nape to her back, then her waist, pulling her in against him again. He saw from the glow in her eyes that she liked what she felt and had wants of her own, though they might be buried under her natural caution. He could understand that, knowing she'd been hurt, knowing it must be hard to trust again.

"Believe me, Liss, I see how this complicates things, but there's not a hell of a lot I could do about it if I wanted to, and I don't want it to stop. Every time I see you, bang! there it is again. It isn't something that's going to go away, and whatever it is, we'd be a hell of a lot more comfortable discussing it in bed."

"No!" Liss shoved her hands against his chest, struggling not to succumb to the desire that urged her to listen to him, to give in to him, to her own needs. "Whatever it is, it will go away if we simply leave it alone, let it die a natural death. We have to share this house, but it doesn't mean we have to share a bed. You have plenty of others you can get that from and—"

"Dammit, I thought we'd disposed of that topic! What if I don't want it from anybody else? What if you are—" He broke off, then went on, leaving her wondering what he'd been about to say.

"I knew before we even got to the lawyer's office that this could happen if we had a chance to be together. Then, because I didn't know what Brose's will would mean to both of us, I tried to ignore it because I live here and you lived there. But now, Liss, we both live here. And we share these feelings. Why, then, shouldn't we share a bed?"

"Kirk . . . " She bit her lip, reminding herself of what he'd said as they'd watched the sunset Monday afternoon. There were no women in his life at his invitation. Yet doubts still assailed her. "I think we should at least try friendship first."

"We can," he said. "We will. Friendship," he whispered roughly, "and this." She sighed and buried her hands in his hair, pulling his head down for her kiss.

Seven

The wafflelike underlay cushioned Liss's back. Kirk's hardness pressed boldly into her as he lifted himself over her, pinning her beneath his weight. The scent of new rubber filled the air, not quite overriding the scent of his skin. Liss knew she should move away, knew she should fight off the numbing desire that weakened her muscles, addled her brain, mesmerized her and kept her right where she was, her arms around his neck, her legs entwined with his. She wanted to deny that she felt as strongly as he did, but she couldn't, not even to herself. Her heart hammered hard and heavily as she dragged her mouth free of his so she could explore the texture and taste of his throat. His voice, low, intense, spoke in her ear, asking, promising, praising. She ached with a terrible intensity for release of the coiling heat that his words, the feel of his body, the scent of his skin, had fired within her. He slid a hand slowly, sensuously from her back to her front, under her shirt, and cupped a breast in his palm. Her nipple sprang erect and she gasped, a sound he captured and contained within the depths of his kiss.

She leaned into his kiss, wrapping her arms around his torso and opening her mouth at his insistent probing. He shifted sideways, undoing her bra and sliding her shirt up. Her entire body quivered at the touch of his fingers on her naked stomach, then her breast. When he captured the hard nipple between his fingers, tugging on it, she moaned; when he bent his head and took her in his mouth, she let her breath out in a silent sob. He reached down and took one of her knees, drawing her leg up, pulling her tight, tighter to his loins. As his hips thrust suggestively, she went hot all over and released a soft, agonized cry of yearning and surrender.

"Harrumph!"

For a moment, neither Kirk nor Liss knew what the sound had been, what it meant, why it was intruding into the sensual heat of their desire. Then, when it was repeated, louder, Liss knew. With a choked gasp, she broke free of Kirk's arms, pulled her shirt down, shoved the rolls of underlay back, scrambled to her feet. She stared in horror at Mrs. Healey, who stood in the doorway, hands on her ample hips, cane dangling from one fist.

"Working hard, I see," she said, pinning Liss under her cold gaze until Kirk, too, arose from the floor, pushing at the pad as it coiled and writhed around him.

"The, uh, underlay wouldn't lie down," Liss said unnecessarily, then wished she hadn't even tried to make excuses. Mrs. Healey simply poked her nose in the air and looked at her down it.

"But you, of course, would?" she said with a sniff. "And with anybody, by the looks of it. Any-where. You ought to be ashamed of yourself, young woman! A widow, a mother, participating in such disgusting, animalistic behavior! Have you no respect for your husband's memory? No respect for the sensibilities of your innocent children, either of whom could have walked in at any moment? You—"

"Now just one minute," Liss said warningly, "my children are upst—"

Mrs. Healey, however, once started, was not about to be silenced. "No! You wait just a minute, young lady! I'm not finished. Take my warning," she went on, waving her cane at Liss. "I won't tolerate any funny business between you two. Ambrose put me here as chaperone for a good reason. I'm a God-fearing, churchgoing woman, and as long as I live here, there'll be no immoral conduct between you two or anyone else in this house."

She lumbered closer and shook her cane under Liss's nose. "If you can't comport yourself with proper dignity, then I'll have no option but to let your in-laws know that you aren't a fit mother—"

"Hey!" Kirk's voice sliced through the diatribe like an ax. He snatched Mrs. Healey's cane and aimed it at the ceiling, rather than at Liss's face. "'Immoral conduct'?" he thundered. "After the way you and Brose lived, you can dare to talk about immoral conduct in others? Listen, you sanctimonious old—"

"Watch it, sonny," she said, wrenching her cane free and poking his belly with it. "When I lived here with Ambrose, there were no children involved."

"For your information, Liss's children were not involved in any way with what we were doing," Kirk said. "They are upstairs asleep in their beds, and what Liss and I do is none of your business. When you saw we were . . . busy, you should have had the decency to keep on going. We are both adults and do not require a chaperone, and I won't put up with any interference from you!"

"Children have been known to wake up," Mrs. Healey said with self-righteous pedantry. She lowered her cane, nonetheless, perhaps intimidated by Kirk's anger. "You wouldn't have heard them coming any more than you heard me."

"My kids make a lot more noise than you do when you choose not to pound your cane on the floor," Liss said. "There's nothing sneaky or snooping about Ryan and Jason."

Mrs. Healey glowered at her. "Mothers need to take extreme care with their actions, especially mothers whose children have grandparents who might be rightfully seeking custody. So I suggest you watch your step from here on, miss. Very, very carefully, because I will be watching, too."

She turned and stumped away.

"Oh, hell, I'm sorry," Kirk said as Liss spun around, turning her back to him. Her shoulders were heaving, and choking sounds came from her throat. "Ah, Liss, don't cry, sweetheart. I won't let her hurt you or your kids. I didn't mean for anything like that to happen, I didn't intend to forget where I was, what I was doing. I'm not saying I'm sorry it happened, only that I'm sorry it happened where it did, and when." He turned her around and lifted her face. "Please, look at me."

Liss opened her eyes and stared up into his misery-filled face. She covered her mouth with a hand, but nothing could stem the giggles that burst forth. "Oh, Kirk! The look on her face! Wasn't it priceless?"

"You're *laughing*?" he exclaimed. "This isn't funny, Liss!"

"It is, it is." She laughed again. "Kirk, please,

don't look so tragic. Not much happened, and what did wasn't your fault. Don't worry about it."

"What do you mean, it wasn't my fault?" he asked, jamming a hand through his hair. "Of course it was my fault! Damn! If that pious old bat makes trouble, do you know what it will mean to—" He broke off and sighed gustily. "I guess I'd better get back to work."

Liss tried not to giggle again, but it bubbled forth in spite of her. "Boy, I bet your carpet-laying manual never covered anything like this either."

He looked at her for another couple of seconds, clearly finding no humor in this situation. "Nothing I've ever read or done or imagined covered anything like this."

He stomped out of the room and returned with the new carpet, which he unceremoniously dumped on top of the underlay. After he'd eased it into position, Liss flattened the loose end to the floor and began to roll it out.

"Hold it away from the tack strip if you can," he said. "I don't want it getting hooked on the tacks prematurely or it will lie crooked."

As he instructed her he picked up what he'd earlier called a "carpet kicker." The rubber-and-metal device, when placed against the carpet surface and rammed with his knee, stretched the rug tight enough so that it reached the wall and could be forced down over the nails in the tack strip.

"Damn her!" He set the carpet kicker into place and slammed his knee into it. "I've punched out more than my share of dirty-minded men and boys for that kind of attitude when it was aimed at my mother, but I've never in my life even considered hitting a woman."

For a moment, as he met Liss's gaze, he looked positively fierce. "I came pretty damned close to wrapping that cane around her neck." He smashed his knee forward and more of the carpet was forced into place. "You bring out some strong primitive instincts in me, Liss Tremayne."

Primitive instincts? she repeated silently. Did those equate with animalistic behavior? Abruptly she felt sick. Kirk was right. There was nothing remotely funny about what had happened. It must have been hysteria making her laugh like a loon. She had never had a purely sexual relationship and hadn't thought she was capable of having one—at least until this afternoon when Kirk's touch, his kisses, his very presence sent her into a sensual haze where edges blurred and she forgot how short a time she'd known this man. Then it hadn't mattered. And it certainly should have! Mrs. Healey, if she chose, could make plenty of trouble for her. What had Kirk been about to say after Mrs. Healey left? What it will mean to whom? To her? To him? It wouldn't affect him at all, except he might feel a certain amount of guilt, which was foolish. Mrs. Healey was right. The woman was the one who had to take care. Kirk should know that, too, as the illegitimate son of a woman who'd probably been blamed all her adult life for her "mistake."

Liss was glad of an excuse to change the subject. "Your . . . your mom had a hard time, didn't she?"

"Yeah," he said. "About as rough as it comes." *Wham!* He kicked the carpet forward again. "A woman with an illegitimate child didn't get a lot of respect in those days. Most people figured she was unwed because the man refused to marry her, but in her case, it was the other way around."

Wham! "She turned him down," he said as he progressed along one side of the room, "even knowing she was pregnant. In fact, she didn't tell him about me because around the time she realized I was on the way, she also realized she couldn't link her life up with Brose's."

Liss frowned. "That couldn't have been an easy decision to make."

"It wasn't, but she's one tough lady, my mom, and I give her all the respect other people—Brose included—denied her." *Wham!* He paused for a moment to line the kicker up again. "You'd never know, looking at her, how strong she really is. Velvet over steel," he said musingly before he rammed the instrument home. "Like somebody else I know."

When Liss failed to respond to the bait, he went on.

"She had to be strong, of course, to make her escape from a man like Brose, who was a human steamroller."

"Why didn't she want to marry him? Didn't she love him?"

He glanced at her, and they turned the corner of the room, heading up the other side as she continued to hold the carpet up a few inches. "Oh, yes, she loved him. But in spite of that, she wouldn't let herself be walked on, and he was determined to make all the decisions about their life." He paused to rub his knee, then resumed the work as well as the story.

"She knew it would be better for her child to be raised in happiness by one strong parent than torn apart by the massive differences in outlook between her and Brose." He glanced at her again. "Much the way you turned down an affluent life and a secure home with your in-laws because it was better for your kids not to be under their influence."

"I don't think your comparison works," she said, uncomfortable with it. They had reached the last few feet of carpet, and he was much too close. She let him have the carpet end and walked across the room, ostensibly to test the depth and texture of the thick, cushiony brown carpet. Kirk was wrong about her, she thought, watching his broad shoulders heave as he forced the carpet down. She wasn't strong. She wasn't tough. Most of the time since she'd left her in-laws' home she'd been teetering on the thin edge of terror—fear for the future, fear that her children's needs weren't being met, fear that someone would look at her and find her seriously wanting in some way, a washout as a mother. Exactly as Mrs. Healey had done today.

"I think the comparison works fine," Kirk said, finishing the last corner of carpet. He left the carpet kicker there and limped over to her. "She refused to marry him because he wouldn't consider a church wedding and that was important to her. Brose had a very low opinion of churches and believed religion in any form was bad. He called it a crutch for the weak. My mother couldn't agree, so she left him." He smiled at Liss. "Too bad Reverend Daisy wasn't around in those days to convert him."

"But then you'd never have known your dad, Martin Allbright," she reminded him.

He slid a hand around her neck. "Neither would I have had a chance to meet you," he said softly, drawing her inexorably closer, as if completely oblivious of their nemesis only a room or two away, and the warning she'd given them.

Liss had not forgotten. She twisted away quickly, dislodging his hand before she could be caught up in the magic web of his touch. "Stop it," she said.

"What's the matter? You're the one who found it funny."

"Now, I don't. Now, I'm scared." She backed away from him.

"Are we going to let that old bat dictate our actions?" he asked, following her. She took another step back. He took one forward. She stepped again—and her back was to the wall. Kirk leaned one hand beside her head and with the other stroked her cheek, her shoulder, her neck, sending her heart rate into a crazy, looping, rising spiral. "Velvet over steel," he murmured. "A strong woman to turn on a strong man."

"No," she whispered.

"Yes. Come on, Liss, admit it. You left a secure home with your in-laws because you thought it would be better for your sons. You came here, despite your misgivings, also because it would be better for them. You were determined to tough it out, to take on a life completely alien to you, and in the process, you discovered how you could make it work for you, found a positive side to it with your photography. You're a survivor, Liss. You're strong, you're tough, and you don't let other people make the important decisions for you."

She laughed bitterly. "If you believe that, why are you trying to make this one for me?"

His denial was quick. "I'm not. You want what we could have together every bit as much as I do."

"I can't give in to feelings like that," she said raggedly. "And I won't, because it would be wrong. A purely sexual relationship isn't for me. I have two children whose happiness is at risk because Olga Healey would like nothing better than to cause trouble. That's something I have to bear in mind every minute of every day."

He leaned closer. His breath was warm on her

face, his eyes dark and intense. "What we're doing isn't wrong. It's important, Liss, to both of us. I don't know yet how important, because it's too soon, but I do know it isn't immoral. We're getting to know each other the way men and women have since time began. How can that be bad?"

She knew he was making sense. She wanted to know him better, to explore the growing emotion between them. It could be so much more than sex. She knew that. She knew, too, that Mrs. Healey was in the wrong, but still she had to acknowledge that the older woman could do a lot of damage.

She slipped under his arm and strode to the center of the room, putting several feet between them.

"No," she said. "My kids are what's important to me. I can't risk their happiness for a moment's pleasure."

"Run away now if you like," Kirk said, "but one of these days you'll realize there's no place left to run, and you're going to have to make good on those silent promises I see in your eyes, city girl."

She swallowed hard. "Don't let your imagination run away with you. My eyes are making no promises or even suggestions to you, because I want more than I know a man like you has to offer a woman."

Her forthrightness sent a sudden jolt through Kirk. For an instant he was the one who wanted to run, because he could almost see himself making her the kind of offer he knew most women wanted to hear. *Let me take you away from all this. . . .* But, hell, "all this" was his life, and a damned good one at that. He had no intention of changing it for anyone, let alone a woman he'd known for less than a week. "Come on, Liss," he said. "Aren't you asking for too much, too soon?"

"No. That's the point. I'm not asking for anything except that you respect my wishes in this. Seems to me you're the one doing most of the asking."

That set him back on his heels, too, because he knew she was right.

Hearing the boys awake in their room, he knew he had only moments more to get this settled. He crowded in close, backing her up to the opposite wall this time. He braced both arms against the wall on either side of her, not touching her, but feeling as if she were pressed against him. "I'm not asking for anything you don't want to give," he said. "For the love of Mike, woman, I've kissed you. I've felt you respond. You want me as badly as I want you. Why not simply give in to those feelings, Liss? They're natural, normal, and damned compelling."

His gaze was compelling, Liss thought. She met it and forced herself to withstand the power of it. He may be strong, as was his desire, his need. And hers! But she would be stronger. Hadn't he said she was strong, tough, a survivor? He might not like it, but there was nothing to prevent her from using that strength to fight him, was there?

With a physical act of will, she forced herself to duck under his arm and flee upstairs, but not to her children. Entering her room, she shut the door and leaned on it, shivering with reaction to all that had transpired during the afternoon.

"What if I don't want it from anybody else?" he'd asked, and the temptation to listen to him had been so great, she'd nearly succumbed. She might have if they hadn't been interrupted. She felt as if she'd narrowly missed slipping over a precipice, and wondered how big a push he would have had to give her before she tumbled into the same abyss as all the other women in his past.

"No," she said aloud. "It will not happen to me. I will not get caught in his trap. I have to provide the cake, but not the kisses. Those, he can get elsewhere."

With Liss's sofa and chairs in place on the new carpet, along with the bookcase and a couple of small tables, and a fire on the hearth, the playroom took on a warm, inviting air.

"Hey, this looks good," Kirk said Friday evening when he poked his head into the room. Liss had just jumped down off a chair, having finished adjusting the drapes. She froze in place, her breath caught in her throat as she looked at him. Dressed in a cream-colored sweater and dark slacks, he carried a jacket over his shoulder, and for the first time since she'd met him, he wasn't wearing cowboy boots but highly polished black loafers. He was on his way out. She swallowed the pain in her throat. After all, she'd told him to respect her wishes and leave her alone. She couldn't complain if he did that, could she? But dammit, he looked great, making her acutely aware of her scruffy jeans and baggy sweater. The woman he was going out with would be dressed nicely, too, casually, as he was, but with quality and flair. Into her mind popped a picture of Gina Holland in her high-heeled boots and tight navy blue leggings.

Kirk leaned on the door frame, his gaze sweeping over her, making her hot and uncomfortable—and making her doubt the wisdom of demanding that he respect her wishes. Because when she looked at him, her wishes took on an entirely different character. She met his gaze for as long as she could, then turned to carry the chair back to a table in the corner, where the boys sat gluing macaroni elbows to sheets of cardboard.

"Come out with me, Liss," Kirk said abruptly, surprising himself. He pushed away from the door frame and followed his instincts across the room to her, feeling drawn by her wary gaze. To hell with "respecting her wishes," he thought. To hell with the caution he'd preached to himself since Wednesday. He wanted to spend time with Liss Tremayne, and he wanted a hell of a lot more than that. A man couldn't be hung for trying, he told himself.

"I was going to meet a couple of friends in the bar," he said, "but I'd rather go someplace with you. We could take in a movie. There might even be a band tonight at the Legion Hall."

Liss thought about sitting at his side in a darkened theater, maybe holding hands, maybe snuggling within the curve of his arm. She allowed herself to think, briefly, of dancing with Kirk. How long had it been since she'd danced? As she'd told him, she'd been out of circulation a long time. With a silent sigh she shook her head. "Sorry. I have plans."

Kirk was taken aback. He couldn't remember the last time he'd been turned down so peremptorily. Hell, yes, he could. He'd been in high school and covered with zits. "Like what?" he asked, remembering the excuse Rhonda Simons had used. "Washing your hair?"

Liss grinned. "No. I did that this morning. I joined the library today."

He blew out a long, frustrated breath. "It's Friday night! How can you contemplate staying home with a library book?"

She had to laugh. He really had no idea, did he,

in spite of being raised by a single mom? "This is how I spend most of my Friday nights. And Saturday nights, too, for that matter. I don't suppose you've got a baby-sitter in your back pocket."

"But Mrs. Healey's here and—" He broke off. "No. I suppose not."

"Right," Liss said. "Absolutely not."

"Okay, then." He flung his jacket onto a chair and sank down on the sofa. Sticking his long legs out in front of him, he toed off his loafers, then, feet on the coffee table, he reached for the top book on her stack. "We'll stay home and read library books together." As he saw alarm leap into her eyes, he decided maybe he'd have to, after all, respect her wishes. But dammit, he'd do it on his terms, not hers. She'd never said they couldn't spend time together, only that he couldn't try to seduce her into his bed.

Liss stared at him. "You don't have to stay home with me."

He took her hand and drew her down beside him. "I know that. But what if I want to, Liss? What if that's what I prefer?"

She could only gaze at him, her heart hammering high in her throat, and watch as he opened her new P. D. James mystery and started reading as if it had been his intention all along to stay home with her. She tugged her hand free but continued to sit there, gazing at the fire, listening to the boys as they argued and the faint sounds of Mrs. Healey's television in the living room, and casting the occasional sideways glance at Kirk's profile.

Fine, she thought after a minute. If he wanted to sit there and read, or if he wanted to watch television, she'd go along with him. But the minute he tried to kiss her, she was out of there! Fast. Running all the way.

• • •

Liss lay in bed later that night and stared up into the darkness. Kirk hadn't read all evening. They hadn't watched television. While she was putting the boys to bed, he'd made hot chocolate and popcorn, and they had spent the next two and a half hours playing Scrabble, talking, laughing. Not once had he tried to kiss her. Not one remotely suggestive word had crossed his lips. He hadn't even given her one of those smoldering glances of his, or the kind of smile that made her insides quiver.

They quivered, though, and her heart even stopped beating, when she heard his steps on the stairs, heard him heading down the hall, heard him pause outside her door. Then he walked on and she started breathing again. Still, it was a long time before she slept, and she didn't wake up until late.

Kirk had taken the boys to Kristy's for their first riding lesson. He'd left a note asking Liss to join them, and giving her detailed instructions on how to get there. She did, and to her amazement she soon found herself astride a horse for the first time since she was six years old. Even more surprising, she thought she might enjoy it once she felt more confident.

What with riding lessons on Saturday, church on Sunday, and dinner at the Fontaines' later that day, the weekend was busy, giving Liss little time to dwell on what had gone before. She took the boys back to school Monday morning, shaking her head at their pleading to be allowed to stay all day, to carry lunch boxes and ride the school bus.

By Wednesday she acceded to at least part of their request and packed lunches for them.

"Can we come home on the school bus?" Ryan begged, his eyes huge and dark under his straight black brows.

She laughed and hugged him. "Not this time, sweetie. When you go to kindergarten next year, then you can ride on the bus. And yes, Jase, the following year, it'll be your turn. You're only staying all day today and tomorrow, and maybe Friday, because I'll be there, too, painting Christmas scenes on classroom windows."

Kirk, who had come into the kitchen for coffee, glanced over at her. "That's good of you, Liss."

She shoved her fingers into the back pockets of her jeans and fixed him with a level gaze. "Yes," she said dryly. "I think so, too, considering that I wasn't the one who all but volunteered my services. It seems somebody told somebody else that I might know one end of a paintbrush from the other."

He tipped his hat to the back of his head. "I wonder who that could have been."

He looked so supremely innocent that Liss had to laugh, watching while he studiously, busily, sorted a handful of nails and screws he'd taken from his jacket pocket and dumped on the counter.

"Quite a mystery, wouldn't you say," she asked, "since I told only one person in this valley about my background?" She poured his coffee and set it on the table. "Of course, you didn't have anything to do with it."

He laughed, his eyes glittering like chips of silver. "Well, I guess maybe I could have mentioned it to Patty. In passing, you know. Just that you'd been to art school. After all, I don't know if you can paint, do I?"

She shook her head solemnly. "No, you don't. Poor kids, they might end up with one-eyed Santas with feet coming out of their ears. You know what crazy things some artists do." She lowered her voice to gossip level. "Especially artists from the city."

He hung his jacket over the back of a chair and flipped his hat to the top of the refrigerator. "No," he said, hooking a chair out with one foot. Instead of sitting down, though, he opened his arms, as if inviting her in. "I don't know what kinds of things artists do. Go ahead. Do something crazy. Show me."

His laughing eyes dared her, and Liss's heart went wild for a long, almost painful moment as she admitted to herself how tempted she was to show him exactly how crazy he could make her feel with nothing more than that smile of his. The smile faded as she met his gaze, and she shook her head as Mrs. Healey's cane thumped along the upstairs hall.

"Ah, Liss . . ." he said softly, his face filled with frustration. She detected a tremor in his fingers as he held out a hand and grasped hers. He tugged gently, and she let him draw her toward him. Lifting her free hand, she slid it up his muscular forearm, over the bulging biceps muscle, and on to his broad shoulders. She reveled in the feel of him, in the desire she saw flare in his eyes. For that brief time, she forgot Mrs. Healey's threats, forgot Kirk's saying *"Aren't you asking for too much, too soon?"* and remembered only the magic they created together each time they kissed. She longed for it again, tenderness for this big, craggy-faced man making her ache. But as Jason came in from the utility room with his coat half on, one sleeve inside out, she stepped back from Kirk and he dropped her hand. The moment was lost.

"I'll drive," Kirk said. He gulped his coffee, grabbed

his jacket and hat, and followed Liss outside. "If you don't mind, that is. I have to go to the lumber-yard."

She tossed him the keys. "I don't mind. I'd let Jack the Ripper drive as long as there was snow on the road."

He grinned. "Powder puff."

Complacently she agreed, and asked what he needed at the lumberyard. He didn't answer until they were all in and buckled up. "Plywood," he said, backing out of the yard. "I figured if I volunteered you to paint the classroom windows, the least I could do was make the scenery they're going to ask you to paint for the upcoming concert."

She stared at him. "You volunteered me to paint scenery, too?"

He shrugged one shoulder. The movement reminded her of the way his muscles had felt under her hand, hard and mobile and warm. . . . *Oh, damn! Keep your mind where it should be,* she told herself. She was fine as long as she didn't dwell on the feel of him, the taste, the scent. . . .

"I didn't exactly volunteer you," he said, cutting into her thoughts. "But Patty thought if she got you involved with doing the windows, it would follow naturally that she could talk you into doing the rest of it." He reached across the seat and touched her cheek. For an instant, he took his eyes off the road and looked into hers. "I'll help you all I can, Liss, and set up a workshop for you in the barn, with plenty of lights and a table for your equipment. It'll be a joint project." Again, he flicked a glance at her. "It's for the kids, Liss."

After a long moment she said, "If it's for the kids, of course I'll do it."

He caught her hand in a loose grip. "Thanks, Liss. You don't mind, do you? Working with me?"

"I don't mind," she murmured.

He turned onto the highway. "Good."

"Because what we'll be doing is working together," she said, emphasizing the verb.

He cast another quick glance at her and smiled faintly. "Of course we will be. Isn't that what partners do?"

She nodded. "Partners," she said, her voice as light as she could make it. "And friends."

Eight

"If I paint the desert scene on one side and the manger scene on the other," Liss said, "then the stage crew can come on between acts and change backdrops easily."

Kirk was standing in the barn with her, reading the program provided by the school. He looked up and smiled at her. "Keep your paint light, artist, won't you, since your partner is the aforementioned stagehand."

"Oh, by all means. I wouldn't want to overwork you." She stepped back from the stage sets. "Kirk, I've been thinking. . . ."

"You're not supposed to think," he said, "especially if you're thinking you don't need me. You're merely supposed to create."

"Ah, yes," she said, laughing. "One can get terribly creative with a whitewash brush." She aimed it at him.

He picked up another wide brush and dipped it into the bucket of wash they were using to seal the plywood panes. "That's true," he said, approaching her. "Let's see how creative I can get. I wonder how you'll look as an old, white-haired lady."

Laughing and feeling brave armed with her dripping bush, Liss stalked him around the stage sets, reaching out from concealment to slap him on the arm with the brush.

"First blood!" she crowed, and he ceded victory to her, holding his brush high so wash dripped down his arm.

Liss was disappointed. "You didn't put up much of a fight, friend."

"How could I? You're so little, you managed to skulk and hide and sneak up on me." He sighed. "No man should ever do battle with a woman. You all fight dirty, just to win."

"I thought the idea of battles was to win them," Liss said, beginning the first of the panels. She poked her head around the end and grinned at Kirk, who'd started working on the other side. "And if that means skulking and hiding and taking advantage of my small stature, then I'll do it."

He stood on tiptoe and looked at her over the top of the backdrop. "You cheat at Scrabble, too."

"I do not!"

"Do so. What kind of sportsmanship is it to ruin your opponent's concentration by leaning back and stretching, shoving your boobs out against your blouse till it looks as if your buttons will pop?"

Liss's jaw dropped. "I never did that!"

"You do it all the time." He dropped back down out of sight and she could hear his brush slapping on the other side of the panels. "And when you drink hot chocolate, you lick your lips. When you eat popcorn, you suck the butter off your fingers. You set out to win by driving me crazy, Liss Tremayne, and don't try to deny it." He came around to her side to dip his brush again, his eyes dancing.

"If you hate it so much," she asked, "why do you insist we play Scrabble or rummy or watch TV or videos together every evening?"

He grinned at her. "Hey, did I say I hate it?" He wiped one finger across the tip of his brush and dabbed white paint on her nose. "Liss, I've never been happier than since you came here. I want to be with you every evening because I enjoy your company. I'm glad that we're . . . friends."

Slowly she smiled. "Me too." And she was.

"Good." He pulled the tail of his shirt out of his jeans and wiped the paint off her nose, then quickly stepped back around the sets.

"There," Liss said twenty minutes later, standing back to admire what they'd accomplished. "I'll give them another coat this evening; then by the time I get back from driving the kids to Kristy's tomorrow morning, they'll be dry enough so I can start the real work."

"You're a very talented lady," Kirk said, leaning over the table and examining her preliminary sketches.

"Thank you," she replied absently. She bent to pick up one of the kittens that had wandered from its nest in Kirk's workshop. Cuddling it under her chin, she carried it back to its mother. The day Mrs. Healey had tripped on a kitten, mama cat and her babies had been banished to the barn. Kirk assured the boys they'd be much safer there, and it was where they belonged anyway.

"You are too," Liss said a minute later, coming out of his shop with one of his carvings. They fascinated her. Carved out of four-inch-thick cottonwood bark, each one was different, yet each had a haunting, almost tortured quality, as if it were a manifestation of a pain that twisted deep within Kirk, a sadness he could symbolize and maybe alleviate in only this way.

He didn't even glance up, but turned another page in her sketchbook. "I am what too?"

She smiled. "Talented, though not a lady. Kirk, why do you hide these things out here?"

His head shot up. When he saw what she was holding he took half a step toward her, then halted. He said nothing, only looked at her warily, and she sensed his deep protectiveness toward his creations, as if he expected her to scoff or jeer at them.

"You do beautiful work," she said. "I hope you don't mind my looking at your carvings."

"If I did," he said, "I'd lock them away somewhere." He sounded so defensive, she knew he wished he had done so.

"Why do you keep them out here?" she asked, returning to his shop to select another carving to admire. "I mean, why not in the house?"

He shrugged and followed her inside. Toeing the litter of cottonwood bark at his feet, he said, "Look at the mess I make. Would you want that in the house?"

"No, but the finished product should be on display, not out here where no one can see it."

"Do you really like them?" he asked diffidently, an odd expression on his face.

It was as if, she thought, he were afraid that at any moment she'd start laughing derisively. His vulnerability sent a surge of tenderness through her, and she smiled again.

"Yes, Kirk. I really like them."

He cleared his throat and touched one of the carvings with the same kind of gentle caress she'd so often felt on her face. Her skin tingled.

"Brose hated them," he muttered. "He said they looked evil."

She picked up the first one she'd held and tilted it to the light. "Oh, never," she said. "But maybe slightly mysterious, as if they aren't quite of this world." She took another from the workbench and looked at it closely. "This one has a decided puckishness, as if it's about to burst into wicked laughter." She smiled at him again. "At someone else's expense. I love it."

Again, that strange expression crossed his face, as if he might be on the verge of snatching his carving out of her hands—or snatching her into his arms. "Would you sell this one to me?" she asked.

He smiled self-consciously. "Don't be silly. If you want it, take it."

She shook her head. "I won't take it unless I can buy it."

"Why not?" he asked, staring at her as if she were some kind of alien creature.

"Because . . ." She bit her lip, searching for words. "Because it's something that . . . didn't exist before you created it. You put a lot of work and time and . . . a lot of yourself into it. That makes it valuable."

He laughed, but without much humor. "To me, maybe, but not to anyone else."

"If you value it, you should expect others to do the same. Since the currency of our society is money, I want to pay you for it. Maybe then you'll start to give your own creations the respect they deserve."

He lifted the carving out of her hands and set it on the bench. "Money isn't our society's only currency."

She read the intent in his eyes. "No?" Her voice

came out in a soft whisper. "What other currency would you accept in payment?"

He touched her scar, and she shivered in anticipation. Why did he always touch her like that as a prelude to kissing her? she wondered. Did he know how deeply it stirred her, know that it sent little tingles along all her nerve endings and made her mouth go dry? "A kiss," he said softly. "Just one kiss."

She smiled even as her heart started a deep, heavy thrumming. It seemed like months since he'd last kissed her. "Only one? Isn't your work more valuable than that?"

His eyes were dark and deep and very, very solemn. "One of your kisses is worth a lot to me, Liss." His voice was husky, vibrating in her bones. As he bent and touched her mouth with his, she wrapped her arms around him and pressed close, feeling a wonderful rightness in this.

"Oh, Lord!" he said raggedly when he at last lifted his head. "What you do to me, woman! Do it again, okay?"

With a sigh so deep it could have been a sob, she linked her hands behind his neck and offered herself to him once more. She parted her lips under his, accepting his tongue and trembling with the force of their desire as it built and built.

"Liss . . . sweetheart . . ." he said hoarsely. Then, with a swift motion that left her breathless, he grasped her waist and lifted her, holding her against him. As if of their own volition, her legs slid around his middle and she clung to him.

"That's better," he said, kissing her quickly again. "You're magic, but you're hell on my neck and back. Why do you have to be so little?"

"I didn't eat my spinach?" she said, rubbing his neck. They both laughed softly, then sobered as he moved her against his body. Liss drew in a long, tremulous breath at the sensations unleashed by his action.

"Kirk . . ."

With a soft groan, he brought his mouth to hers again. He kissed her slowly and sensuously, rocking her against the hardness of him, showing her his desire and feeding hers. When he lifted his head, her eyes were glowing with a luminosity that took his breath away.

"Kirk . . ." she said again, and he murmured something incomprehensible in reply. Holding her with one hand under her bottom, he reached out with the other to shut the door. Turning, he then sat down on the bench, cradling her as he tilted her back in his arms, his lips trailing down her throat to the neckline of her sweater while one hand cupped her breast.

She cried out softly, and he whipped her sweater off over her head, then unbuttoned her blouse, all the while watching her face for signs that she wanted him to stop. Her eyes were closed, her breathing shallow, her lips moistly parted and red from his kisses. Her eyes fluttered open as the cool air touched her skin, and she smiled, slowly, sweetly, inviting him to continue. With trembling fingers, he slipped her blouse from her shoulders and down her arms. His lips adored the silk of her skin. His tongue followed the high curve of one breast, then, as he pushed her bra aside, flicked over a cresting nipple. He breathed in the scent of her, then felt her hair brush over his hands and wrists as she arched to his mouth and moaned her pleasure.

Liss felt as if her head were full of thick wool. She was dimly aware that the low, sensual sound she heard when Kirk's mouth closed over her nipple emerged from her own throat. Clenching her hands in his hair, she shuddered at the sweet, pulling sensations of his suckling. When he lifted his head to mutter gutturally, "Woman, what are you doing to me?" she didn't have an answer.

All she could do was clasp her arms around his neck and offer her lips for his kisses again. His hands curved around her breasts, making her ache with a need for more and more. She slid slowly, seductively against his hardness, until he gasped and held her completely still, breathing raggedly against her neck.

"What am I going to do about you?" he asked moments later, lifting her off his lap and setting her beside him. He held her face between his hands as he stared—or maybe glared, she thought—at her, looking as tortured as one of his carvings, and as hard. "You're scaring me, driving me crazy, and I can't find a way to make you stop."

Her stop? It was up to her to stop? Did he think it scared her any less? She wrenched herself free and got unsteadily to her feet, clutching her blouse to her chest. "If you want me to stop, then don't start things," she said angrily.

He stood and snatched her back into his arms, pressing her head to his chest and running a rough, unsteady hand over her bare back.

She wanted never to leave his arms, but before she could give in to the lethargy creeping over her, she pushed him away. "No. Let me go!"

"Ah, Liss, don't be mad at me." He pulled her back against him. "I can't let you go now." He strained her closer, closer, then sank down onto the thick pile of straw beside mama cat's nest as his legs gave way. "I want you so bad!"

Liss wanted him no less, but how could it be? There were too many questions echoing in her mind, too many doubts in her heart. Was she in love with him? No! She couldn't be. There hadn't been enough time. For the same reason, he couldn't be in love with her, and a relationship based on expediency was not right for her. She met his ardent gaze with a troubled one. Cakes and kisses? Supper and sex? What did he want of her?

"Liss . . . I know what you're thinking, sweetheart." He buried his face in her hair and rocked her back and forth. "I keep thinking of the same thing, but remember, Mrs. Healey . . . nobody, has to know what happens between us in private. Make love with me, Liss. I need you so much!"

The straw prickled at the back of her neck as he laid her down, and with a cry, she wrenched herself free. Leaping up, she turned her back and pulled her sweater on over her head before facing him again, her blouse and bra balled up in one fist. "What you're saying is you want a nice little roll in the hay!"

He shot to his feet. "No! Dammit, you make it sound so cheap and tawdry, and what I feel isn't like that at all."

"No?" She kicked at the pile of straw. "What is it you feel, Kirk?"

"Frustrated as hell!" he said, pounding a fist into the other hand. "What do you want me to say, Liss? I don't know what I feel. What do you feel?"

"I don't know either, but I do know that I'm not looking for casual sex. Now, excuse me, please. It's time to pick up the boys."

When she got back, Kirk had gone out, and he didn't return before she finally fell asleep that night—if he returned at all. He was there when she went downstairs Saturday morning, though, cooking oatmeal for the boys, who were eager for their next riding lesson. "I'll take them over," he said. "I know you have the backdrops to do."

"Thank you," she said. She could be as cool and offhand as he.

"Mind if I watch?" Kirk's voice shattered the stillness of the barn and startled Liss. She whirled around.

"I thought you were with the boys!"

"They're with Kristy. She's heading into town after their lesson, so she'll drop them off on her way. I came back to see if you needed any help, and to tell you I'm sorry for getting out of line yesterday. Forgive me?"

It would be so easy to say no, she thought, to tell him to get lost. But she had to be fair. "Yesterday was a . . . mutual thing."

"But I'm the one who asked for too much."

She shrugged. "Not without encouragement. Now, can we drop the subject? There's no point in rehashing it."

He watched her for a moment or two, his eyes narrowed as if he were assessing whether she meant what she said. "Okay," he said at last. "Now, how can I help?"

"You can't help."

"Then may I watch, or will it bother you?"

Dammit, she thought, she'd missed his companionship the previous evening. She'd missed the camaraderie that had been building between them. She'd missed him. With a silent sigh, she turned to smile at him. "Sure. Stick around and watch. It won't bother me at all. When I was in college, I used to paint in Stanley Park, with a wandering audience of thousands. If I could forget they were there, I'll soon forget you're here. Just one rule. No talking to me."

"Okay. Terms accepted." As she glanced at him over her shoulder, curious about the laughter in his tone, he added, "Somebody has to make sure the city-girl artist doesn't do anything outrageous."

How different it was, she mused as she turned back to the panel, dealing with a man who didn't see her talents as unfair competition to his own. But then, why would he? Their talents lay in totally opposite directions. She sighed as she remembered the previous day, what her admiring his carvings had led to.

Get to work, she ordered herself. *Stop thinking about him!* Picking up a brush, she stared at the blank whitewashed panels, then began painting the outlines of tall buildings for the city scene. Her broad strokes soon created windows and doors and ledges and snowy rooftops. With a light brush she sketched in the shapes of people standing on the sidewalk, looking down from windows, hanging wreaths, shaking rugs. She painted cars of a different era, and old-fashioned street lamps. She'd almost made good her promise to forget Kirk was there when he began a rhythmic clip-clop sound with the heel and toe of one boot on the wood floor of the barn floor, and from Liss's brush emerged the sketch of a horse and wagon.

She realized what she was doing and clenched her teeth, but finished it anyway and began on a striped barber pole. Through the window of the shop the traditional barbershop quartet was visible, songbooks in hand. Finished, she went on to a chubby butcher, who stood in the doorway of his meat store, his apron stretched over his big tummy, his shirt sleeves held up with black-and-red-striped bands. Behind her, Kirk shifted positions and stretched, yawning loudly.

To her annoyance, the butcher finished up with one hand covering his mouth. He was yawning.

Several minutes later, as she was refining the characters in the upper-story windows of the buildings, Kirk began humming a recognizable tune. Liss found herself painting large silver bells across the front of a building. That was all right, she assured herself, because, after all, the thrust of this particular piece of scenery was the Christmas song about silver bells. Still, it irritated her to have him force her hand this way.

Kirk got off his stool and walked up behind her, peering at one of the people she'd painted earlier. "That fat one shaking the mop looks like you-know-who."

"Really?" Liss said, forgetting she'd told him not to talk to her. She took a step back to see if he was right, and ran into the wall of his chest. At once, his arms came around her, and she felt his breath on the side of her face as her own escaped her in a whoosh.

"Have you forgotten yet that I'm here?" he asked.

"Of course," she said, wishing she could slow her racing heart. "At least I had, until you spoke."

He turned her in his arms and she could see the laughter in his eyes. "Liar."

"Well, I've been trying to."

He sobered. "I know the feeling. I've been doing the same thing, Liss. It hasn't worked."

"Don't, Kirk. It's easier if we don't give in to this."

"No," he said. "It gets harder and harder. I see you and I want to kiss you. I watch you at work and I want to make you stop and pay attention to me. I lie in bed at night thinking about you only three doors away. I'm slowly going out of my mind because everything about you calls out to me with every breath I take and I have to . . ." His lips brushed over hers, lightly, teasingly. "Kiss you again . . ." Her eyes fluttered closed as he nuzzled under her ear. "Right now . . ."

"Stop it," she said weakly, wanting it never to stop. She liked the feel of his lips, firm and cool as they swept over hers, with a hint of the heat she knew was inside. She shivered with the desire to claim what he offered. He captured her face between his hands and kissed her long and hard and hot, and she melted into him, accepting the heat, offering her own, lifting her arms to his shoulders, pressing herself to his body, straining to get closer, closer, warmer. . . .

They both heard the sound of a car's tires crunching on the dry snow. With a deep sigh of reluctance, he set her back from him.

"Here comes Kristy with the kids," he said.

Liss shoved her shaking hands into her pockets and turned back to the set. "Oh, Lord, and I'm not even nearly half finished!"

"I'll keep the boys occupied for the rest of the day so you can keep working." He glanced at the backdrops. "Don't worry, I'll make sure you have enough free time to have those ready by Monday night."

The backdrops were ready by Monday morning, and as Liss took her place in the audience that night, she gazed at her work with a critical eye. One of the three camels in the wise-men scene looked decidedly drunken, she thought, although when Kirk took the aisle seat beside her, he assured her they were all the most beautiful camels ever.

She laughed at the delightful slipups of the tiny actors, cringed at the crashes from behind the curtains as Kirk and another man turned the scenery between acts, and gratefully accepted compliments on her work. She smiled, thinking how lucky she and her sons were to have landed in such a warmly welcoming community, and she knew deep happiness as the concert drew toward its close. She sat back, watching the children file onstage to take their places for the final songs in front of her city scene. The smallest, Liss's two included, sat cross-legged at the very edge of the makeshift stage in front of the larger children.

As the first soft chord of a carol rose from the piano offstage and childish voices sang the words of "It Came upon a Midnight Clear," her throat tightened. They looked so angelic, all of them, but her two most of all, their dark eyes wide and innocent beneath their straight bangs, pink mouths moving in song. She knew she could pick out their voices over all the others, and her heart swelled to massive proportions, filled with love and pride and joy. *They are so beautiful!* she thought, and thanked God for them.

Kirk's hand tightened convulsively on hers, almost painfully. She glanced sideways at him, then stared, watching as first one, then another, silver teardrop rolled slowly down his face.

As if he heard her silent gasp, he looked at her and grinned crookedly. Leaning close, he wiped his face on the shoulder of her red wool dress, then whispered, "You weren't supposed to see that."

"Well, I did," she whispered back. "What's wrong?"

"Nothing. It's simply that . . . I . . . Oh, hell, I feel so damned *proud* of those two little guys! Look at them up there! They're wonderful. How can you stand it?"

Someone behind them said, "Shh," as Liss gazed wonderingly at him. Kirk was proud of her boys? He shared her feelings? She felt as if he'd handed her the most valuable gift of her life. It was no wonder she loved him so much, she thought, then swiftly straightened, snatching her gaze from his face and staring blindly ahead. She did? She loved him? Oh, yes! She didn't know how it could be, because only a few days ago she'd assured herself that love couldn't happen that fast, but it had. In less than three weeks, she had fallen in love with this man.

She wanted to stand up and shout it to the audience, to the world. She wanted to cuddle against Kirk and whisper it to him alone. She wanted to go away somewhere quiet all by herself and let the reality of it seep through every pore of her being, until it didn't feel so big and so frightening and so wonderful. The more she thought about it, though, the bigger and more frightening and more wonderful it became, and she thought she might explode right where she sat.

As the lights came up, she realized Kirk's gaze was locked with hers. Slowly she focused on him.

"Are you all right?" he asked.

She nodded. "I'm fine." Her voice sounded rusty, as if she hadn't used it in years.

He lifted a lock of hair back from her face. "You sure? You're pale."

She smiled and gently linked her fingers with his, hoping he wouldn't ask why she trembled. "I'm sure."

"Mom! Mommy! Look what we have!"

The boys' calls brought Liss whirling from where she stood at the stove stirring the thick, rich chicken stew she'd made for dinner the day after the concert.

Ryan and Jason raced through the back door ahead of Kirk—the three of them had left on a mysterious mission more than an hour ago—and when he staggered in under the weight of an enormous evergreen tree, Liss's jaw dropped. "Isn't it huge?" Ryan said, his eyes dancing.

Liss gulped. "I'll say!"

Jason touched its prickly branches as Kirk dragged it into the kitchen and tried to stand it erect. It was too tall even for the nine-and-a-half-foot ceiling of the old ranch house. He settled for angling it against the wall and held it with one hand while he tugged off his boots and jacket with the other.

"Smell it, Mommy!" Jason buried his face in the branches, eyes aglow. "It's for Christmas. We finded it wiff Kirk. Ryan and I picked it out and Kirk cut it down wiff an ax and we towed it home behind the snowmobile. It bounced and turned over and over. I wanted to ride on it but Kirk said no."

Liss hugged her youngest, then sniffed the tree. Its scent had quickly permeated the entire kitchen. "Mmm," she said in genuine appreciation. "It's a wonderful tree." She unzipped Jason's jacket and tugged it from his arms, then helped him out of the bottom half of his snowsuit.

Ryan turned his jacket half inside out getting rid of it, then, little brother in tow, went back to the utility room to hang it up and neatly put boots away. Even now, Santa might be watching.

"Do you really like it?" Kirk asked when they were alone.

"It's a beautiful tree," she said, and he smiled at her, as pleased as a child himself. Grinning, she added, "The question is, where are we going to put it? In the middle of the calving barn?"

Kirk chuckled. He stepped out from behind the huge tree and closer to her, much closer. "They really wanted one about twenty feet tall."

"This one isn't?" she asked weakly, looking up at top of the tree bent against the high ceiling.

The two of them shared a smile that set Liss's heart thundering. The long look he gave her left her breathless, filled with questions, and pulsing with tension that coiled in her belly and weakened her knees.

"Come here," he said roughly, sliding his hand around the back of her neck. He drew her into the shelter of the tree's limbs, hiding the two of them from the children, who were playing with the dog in the entry. "Every time you look at me like that, I want to kiss the living daylights out of you, city girl."

Liss couldn't reply. She could only look at him— probably making those silent promises again, she thought, judging by the way his eyes glittered— and draw in deep breaths laden with the scent of fresh-cut evergreen, resin, and Kirk. Why did the term "city girl" sound so much like an endearment now, when at first he'd used it as an insult? And why did his calling her that make her go all mushy and hot inside? Because she loved him, she thought. She loved him so much. Oh, Lord, what was she going to do if he got tired of her and wanted her out of his life, started treating her the way he treated Gina? She'd leave. She'd have to leave. To her horror, tears flooded into her eyes before she could control her emotions.

"Hey!" Alarm filled Kirk's face. "What's this?"

She blinked and the tears rolled down her face. With a self-conscious laugh, she brushed them away. "Nothing. No, really," she added when he gave her a questioning scowl. "I'm simply feeling . . . sentimental." Quickly she fled back to the stove, leaving him standing there with the tree, the width of the room between them—and a long list of unspoken wishes.

They were still looking at each other from their separate corners when Mrs. Healey entered from the other side of the kitchen. Liss turned at the sound of a disgruntled snort.

"What is that thing doing in here?" Mrs. Healey demanded, thumping her cane on the floor. "*Ambrose* never had a tree in this house."

"Too bad," Kirk said, thumping the trunk of the tree right back at her with a much more impressive thud. "Because we are."

"You aren't putting it in the living room, I can tell you that much, young man! Needles in the carpet, tinsel dropping, and ornaments breaking if you so much as look at them. That big dog of yours could wipe out the entire thing with one sweep of his tail, and the whole mess will dry out and become a fire hazard. It's foolishness, that's what it is, and has nothing to do with the real spirit of Christmas."

"Bah, humbug," Kirk said. He lifted the monster tree onto his shoulder and, with Liss, Ryan, and Jason following, crowded past Mrs. Healey and led the way to the playroom. "Right after dinner, we'll decorate it, okay?" he said as he leaned the tree against the wall. The boys nodded, their eyes alight with excitement.

"With what?" Mrs. Healey, who had trailed after them, asked. "Like I said, Ambrose never had a tree, so what will you do for ornaments?"

Liss smiled at her. "Don't worry, Mrs. Healey. I brought all of mine, and the boys made more at school." She paused. "But even at that, with a tree so huge, we probably won't have enough. Would you like to help us make popcorn strings tonight?"

Mrs. Healey backed up a step or two. "Me?" She sounded appalled. "Why would I want to do that?"

"I don't know," Liss said. "Other than it's Christmas and families normally do things together at this time of year. Kirk and the kids found the tree. The least you and I can do is make sure it's decorated." She felt Kirk's startled gaze on her and couldn't meet his eyes.

"Hmmph!" Mrs. Healey snorted. "Families! I could tell you a thing or two about families, miss."

"I'm sure you could, and I could tell you a few things, too. But I'm certain my idea of family and yours are so far apart, we'd bore each other." She took her children's hands. "Come on, guys. Let's eat so we can get at the tree."

As they left the playroom Liss noticed that Mrs. Healey drew in a deep breath of the evergreen scent, and even looked slightly less austere for just a moment, maybe even a tad wistful. However, she took herself off to the office and her precious accounts after dinner, leaving the decorating of the tree to those who would enjoy it.

"Here," Kirk said to Liss as he prepared to set up the tree. "There's mail. I forgot it earlier." He handed her a sheaf of envelopes. She glanced at them idly, then pounced on one, ripping it open and letting out a shriek of pure joy.

"What's wrong?" Kirk demanded, letting the tree crash to the floor as he hurried to her side.

"I did it! I did it!" she cried, spinning around. "Look! It's a check!" She flung her arms high, then kissed the check. "Oh, Kirk! I did it! Graham's sold some of my stuff. It's like a miracle," she said, subsiding onto the sofa. "I feel free again. I feel . . . like a real person. I feel as if I can do anything now, go anywhere, that there are no more limits!"

"I'm . . . happy for you, Liss," he said, and she looked at him sharply.

He was smiling, but she knew he was not happy for her. He was lying through his teeth. Unbidden came the memory of Johnny looking exactly the same way when she'd made a particularly exciting sale, as if her talent, her success, somehow undermined him.

Kirk seemed to sense disappointment, for he sat down beside her and gave her a hug. "It's great news, Liss," he said, this time smiling genuinely, "and I'm very, very proud of you."

She met his gaze for a moment, seeking reassurance, and to her pleasure, finding it. "Thank you," she said, tucking the check back into its envelope. "It isn't really all that spectacular a check," she confessed. "Less than three thousand dollars, but . . ."

"But it's yours and you earned it." He dropped a kiss on her nose. "Congratulations, Liss."

It was hers, she told herself, and she had earned it, and she wasn't going to let his momentary sullenness detract from her joy in it. Returning his hug, she laughed up at him. "Don't we have a tree to decorate tonight?"

Nine

Kirk took such great pains to get the tree exactly centered in the big window facing the highway, and then the strings of lights so perfectly balanced, Liss finally gave up and left him to it. "You're a perfectionist," she said, as she refilled their eggnog glasses from the jug on the coffee table. "What does it matter if there are two red lights side by side? It's not as if we're going to have tour buses stopping to view our display."

He smiled at her over his shoulder. "I take Christmas seriously, city girl. Tour buses! Don't we deserve perfection, too, even if the world isn't going to be driven to our door to ooh and aah?"

"If you say so," she murmured, sitting back down on the sofa to watch and to string popcorn. "As long as you don't expect me to help you achieve that flawlessness and symmetry."

He chuckled. "As if any mere woman could."

She returned his smile. "If you're trying to challenge me to help you, you're out of luck."

"You're lazy," he said.

She nodded happily, then sipped her spicy drink

and got back to work on the popcorn and cranberries. Presently she set a completed string down and closed her eyes, listening to the sounds of a family Christmas—the children squabbling, the "daddy" grumbling at a recalcitrant string of lights, carols playing in the background while a fire crackled on the hearth. It was wonderful and dreamlike and completely unreal, but nobody had yet made fantasies illegal. Her first major sale in four years was simply a bonus, and she could weave fantastic dreams about what that would mean, too.

She opened her eyes when Kirk sat down beside her. "There now, isn't that a fine-looking tree?" he asked, nodding in smug approval.

"It's a beautiful tree," she said. "Or it will be, when we hang the rest of the ornaments."

"It's a beautiful tree now," he said as he snatched her pillow. He smacked her on the head with it, then stuffed it behind his own head. "The prettiest I've seen, and that's because it has a couple of kids sprawled under it."

She pulled up one leg and wrapped her arms around it, then rested her cheek on her knee. "Were you a lonely child, Kirk?"

He thought for a moment while he drank half his eggnog. "I never realized it until I saw those two together, but I guess so." He toyed with the pink ribbon holding back Liss's hair. "I had plenty of friends, so I wasn't what you might call a solitary kid, but I guess I was a bit lonely at times. Were you?"

She nodded, and the ribbon pulled free, spilling her hair onto her back and shoulders. Kirk filtered his fingers through it, taking pleasure in the texture of it, admiring the way her silky black hair looked against her pink angora sweater.

"There's a special relationship between siblings," she said, "that only children miss out on no matter how many good friends they have. Maybe that's why I was so eager to have two close together."

Kirk lifted a handful of her hair and let it trickle slowly out of his fingers. "What you said earlier, about what 'families' do together at Christmas. I liked that. I felt . . . included, whether you meant me to or not."

"I'm glad you didn't mind. I regretted saying it," she admitted softly. "I thought maybe you'd think I was being presumptuous."

"Never." He wrapped a lock of her hair around his right forefinger and smoothed it with his thumb, concentrating on it; then he glanced at her. "Liss, speaking of families . . ."

"What?"

"I know I should have told you this sooner, but I was afraid you'd object and . . . well, my mom is coming for Christmas."

She met his gaze with surprise. "Object? Why would I? This is your home. If anybody raises a fuss, it'll be you-know-who." She frowned and shook her head to dislodge his hand from her hair. "I only hope your mother can look after herself."

"She can." He handed her ribbon to her as she bunched her hair back again. "She'll probably even knock a few corners off the old bat."

"We can but hope," Liss said doubtfully.

Glancing at her watch, she saw it was time for the children to be in bed. Jumping to her feet, she herded them upstairs. When she returned half an hour later, Kirk met her with a bowl of mandarin oranges, a plate of butter tarts she'd made, and a fresh glass of eggnog for each of them.

"Come and curl up here," he said, patting the couch at his side. "Let's get cozy."

"Nope." She grabbed a butter tart off the plate and evaded his hand by dancing away to pick up a box of ornaments. "No time for that. We have to get the tree finished so we can have this house looking as if we mean to celebrate Christmas, or Lord knows what your mother will think about your new partners. Come on, lazybones, get that ladder in operation."

Kirk laughed as he unfolded the stepladder for her. He held it while she climbed it, then handed her a box of glass balls. Tenderness softened his smile. She was nervous, he thought. About what? The thought of his mother coming? He wanted to pull her into his arms and comfort her and tell her it would be all right. She wouldn't meet his gaze, though. She kept busy, hanging one ornament after another, then asking for another box. All right, he decided. If this was the way she needed to handle her anxieties, he'd help her.

"I know what my mother's going to think of one of my partners," he said, handing her the star.

"Yeah?" She reached high, trying to put it on the top of the tree. He placed a hand in the small of her back for support.

"Liss, *my* mom's going to like you," he said, then blinked at the emphasis he'd put on the pronoun. It was, he told himself, only because he remembered the wounded look in her eyes when she'd said the McCalls didn't like her because of her "mixed blood." It was important that she know his mother wasn't like that, but she pretended she wasn't concerned.

"That's good," she said lightly. She tilted her face toward the ceiling, listening to the boys still fooling around in their beds, or more likely, not in their beds. "I only hope your mother likes kids.

Those two aren't going to settle down now until after the big day."

"She does," he said, moving to the other side of the tree to begin decorating there. Through the branches he noted the way the twinkling lights reflected in Liss's eyes and put roses in her cheeks. "And she's going to think your kids are as special as I do."

"You know," she said, parting some twigs to smile down at him, "I've never been more touched than I was when you said you were proud of my boys."

"I was. I am. They looked so great up on that stage, so . . . beautiful." His throat choked up, and he wanted to tell her he wasn't going to let her take them away, any more than he was going to let her leave, no matter how much she earned with her photography. But he didn't have the right to say any of that. They were partners, as she so frequently reminded him, friends at best. If he was going crazy from wanting more than that from her, he couldn't ask for it unless he asked for the whole ball of wax.

Sighing, he finished his box of ornaments, then turned to get another, but he got distracted by the butter tarts. Standing there eating them one after another, he watched Liss's slender body stretch and reach as her dainty hands hung the ornaments; watched her head tilt to one side as she considered one position for a ball, then moved it to another. Then, when she reached too far, she teetered, one arm flailing, and cried out— his name. He dived for her, shouting, "Liss!" He caught her and dragged her off the ladder into his arms.

"Oh, sweetheart, you're all right, you're safe, I

caught you," he said, his legs shaking so hard he had to sit down and cradle her on his lap.

"Of course I'm all right," she said, gazing up at him, then staring intently. "How about that? I've never noticed before that you have freckles."

He looked at her uncomprehendingly. "Freckles?" Lord almighty, didn't she realize how close a call she'd had? If he hadn't caught her, she'd have fallen and hit her head on the corner of that heavy oak coffee table. The thought made his stomach lurch, and he held her even closer, wanting to protect her, keep her from harm, slay all her dragons, and . . . Good Lord! It hit him then, smacked him between the eyes, stunned him, made his head reel. "Liss," he croaked. "Oh, my God, Liss . . ."

"You do," Liss said. "Across your nose and cheeks." She touched them with her fingers, realizing as she did why she'd never seen them before. He was pale, as white as milk, and his hand trembled violently as he brushed her hair back from her face. "Darling, what is it?" she asked.

"You're not going to leave!" he exclaimed. "I can't let you leave! You're going to stay right here, Liss Tremayne, and marry me if it's the last thing I ever make anybody do and— What did you call me?"

"Darling." She looked guilty and shocked. "What did you say?"

"Marry me." He looked stunned, disbelieving.

For a long moment they stared at each other, both caught in a myriad of swirling, conflicting emotions that clamored within them. Abruptly, though, everything became perfectly clear for Kirk, as if all the questions had been asked and all the answers given. Of course! he thought. It was so simple. He wondered why he had spent so much time arguing with himself, why he had bothered with the doubts and the fears and the confusion, the inner fighting against Brose's apparent intentions for him and Liss. Brose, in spite of his high-handed manipulations, had known what he was doing after all!

He threw back his head and laughed as exultation flooded through him. Then, standing, he spun Liss around and around until she was dizzy and giddy and clinging to him, gasping for breath. He flopped back down on the couch with her, still laughing.

"What's the joke?" Liss asked, still wondering if she had really called him "darling" as if she had the right. And had he really said "Marry me"?

"No joke," he said, planting little kisses all over her face. "Or if there is one, it's on me." He took long enough to kiss her mouth, then looked into her eyes. He seemed bemused, she thought, still half disbelieving of something that was a whole lot clearer to him that it was to her. "He won," he said. "I can't believe it. The old son-of-a— Son-of-a-gun, he *won*!"

"Who?" Liss planted her hands on Kirk's shoulders and tried to shake some sense into him. It was like trying to shake a concrete pillar. "Who are you talking about?"

"Brose!" he said, lying flat and holding her securely atop him. "I fell into his trap, and now I know it's exactly where I want to be. He was right all along. I needed you in my home, I need you in my life. I need you, period." He tightened his arms around her. "Oh, sweetheart, please say you'll marry me!"

Before she could say anything, though, he rolled over, tucking her under him and then kissing her as if he never meant to stop. She grazed his face with her fingertips, his wonderful, beloved face, and knew there were no words for her to tell him what she felt. All she could do was kiss him back.

"I love you," she whispered. "I've known it since the night of the concert when you said you were proud of my kids. Do you know how important that is to me?"

He let out a long, agonized breath. "Do you have any idea how important you have become to me in three weeks?"

"No," she said. "Show me."

"Liss . . ."

He held himself up on one elbow, curving his hand around her face. Her insides curled and twisted in a spasm of hungry response as his mouth touched hers, skimming her lips, making her burn with need. Her hips thrust involuntarily against him as he slipped his hand up under her sweater and cupped her breast. His harshly rasping breath thrilled her before she stole it with a series of tiny, tantalizing kisses that covered his cheeks and throat and ears.

"Kirk," she said, meeting the stormy need in his gaze. "Oh, Kirk, please . . ."

He rejoiced at her willing, giving response, in the hard thrust of her nipple into his palm, the unharnessed hammering of her pulse as his lips found it in her throat.

"Please, please . . ."

Her soft whispers filled him with enormous power and immense pleasure. When he lifted his head and looked down at her, he saw her through a haze of desire, and saw that desire reflected back at him. In that moment, the power went out, plunging the room into darkness.

Liss didn't care. His lips were hard, his tongue was hot and firm as it thrust inside her mouth. His arms encircled her fiercely, dragging her tight against him. The electricity that had left the wires seemed to whip through her, making her shudder and stiffen into a quivering bow of sensation. Gasping, she clung to Kirk, making soft little cries that only inflamed him more.

He kissed her deeply again and again, his hand moving from one breast to the other, fingering her nipples, then skimming down over her waist to the top of her jeans and lower, over her zipper, his fingers curling in between her thighs.

"I want you," he whispered. "I want you right now. I want you to be all mine."

"Yes," she murmured, unbuttoning his shirt and sliding her hands across his chest. She moved again, thrusting against his hand, aching with a need she feared would never be adequately filled and driven by something beyond her control to seek that fulfillment.

The lights flashed on again. Moaning, Kirk sat up and rolled away from her, then dropped to his knees on the floor. Crouching by her side, he stroked her hair, her face, his eyes dark and serious. "No, love," he said. "Stop. We're both forgetting something—someone. I won't put you or your kids at risk. We'll wait, Liss. Wait until we're married."

Slowly she sat up, her eyes big and shocked as her gaze clung to his face. "Married?" she echoed, as if she'd never heard the word before, as if it had no meaning for her.

"Of course, married," he said impatiently. "Didn't you hear me asking you?"

She drew in a deep breath and released it slowly. "I heard," she said, then nothing else.

He waited for as long as he could, holding her face between his hands, looking into her eyes and wishing he could see into her soul. "I didn't hear your answer, Liss."

"I didn't give you one."

"Then hurry up and do it." He dropped his hands to her shoulders. "Liss, don't refuse me, love, please. Marry me."

"I . . . Kirk, why?"

"Why?" His gaze sharpened, but she lowered her eyes and hid her emotions. "Because that's what a man and a woman do when they're in love."

"Is it? How many times have you thought you loved someone? How many times have you considered marriage?"

He let her go and drew his legs up, wrapping his arms around them. "There have been other . . . relationships," he said slowly, carefully. He didn't want to make any mistakes. "You know that, Liss. It would be stupid for me to pretend otherwise. But until I met you, I wanted to stay a bachelor. Hell, until *tonight* I thought I wanted to remain single."

Liss wanted to ask him, *And why don't you now? Is it because you want the cakes as well as the kisses, and with my check's arrival, you can see having to replace the maker of the cakes?* The kisses he could have gotten from Gina. Why hadn't he married Gina, who wanted it so much she risked making herself a laughingstock? Was it because she couldn't cook, because she'd never be content as a rancher's wife?

Oh, Lord, what was the matter with her? Liss wondered. There should be more joy than doubts, yet here she sat, unable to tell him she wanted to be his wife when she did. She did!

"So what's the difference this time?" she asked.

"Liss . . ."

Kirk's pain-filled eyes called out to her to ease his

agony, make it right for him, for them, but how could she when she didn't know what was right for herself? A few days ago, she would have known. But since then, she had seen his face change when she received her check, and out of the blue, he'd said he wasn't going to let her go, that he wanted to marry her. Only belatedly had he said anything about love.

"I can't tell you what the difference is this time because I don't know," he said. "I know only that I want you to be my wife, and I've never wanted that from anybody else."

Kirk watched her face, looked deeply into her eyes, hoping, praying, for a lessening of the doubts, the uncertainty, even the distrust he saw there. If she loved him as he loved her, wouldn't this be what she wanted, too? Didn't a woman know as quickly as a man when everything was exactly right? Didn't women traditionally have a deep-seated need to belong, one they often accused men of lacking?

He thought momentarily of other women he'd known. They'd been the ones to want commitment, the ones with the nesting instinct, and he'd been the one to shy away. But . . . Liss had been married before. She'd had two children with her husband. Maybe her nesting instinct was all used up. As for a home, she had one here, whether she married him or not. And, with her photography business shaping up, she'd soon have enough money to escape this "godforsaken wilderness."

No! The word was a loud cry within him. He couldn't let that happen. He wouldn't! Somewhere, somehow, he'd find a way to convince her. Drawing in a deep, unsteady breath, he got to his feet, then reached for her hands and pulled her up.

"You do love me, don't you? You weren't simply carried away by . . . by . . ."

"I love you," she whispered, her fingers locked with his. "I love you so much, but . . . I—I guess I expected more time before we discussed the future."

As she said them, Liss recognized the validity of her words. Of course, she thought. All these doubts had beset her because she simply didn't know him well enough. She tried to smile, and failed. "It's only been three weeks, Kirk," she said, a wobble in her voice.

"That's time enough for me, Liss." He lifted one of her hands up to his mouth and pressed a kiss into her palm, his eyes never leaving her face. "Can't you recognize in me what I see in you? A life's mate? The life's mate?"

"I think so. I hope so. But I don't know, and I must, Kirk, because I can't help remembering that I knew Johnny for two years before we married and . . ." She swallowed the tears that clogged her throat and looked down at their hands linked so tightly together. "I realized, when he killed himself, that I'd never really known him at all." She lifted her gaze to his face again. It was set in a drawn mask reminiscent of the haunted figures he carved. "If he loved me, how could he have done that? Why wasn't I enough? Where did I fail?"

Kirk squeezed his eyes shut for an instant and pulled her against him. "*I* love you," he said, wishing he knew stronger words to convince her. "With every cell that makes me me, I love you, and I'd never betray you in that way or in any other."

She trembled in his arms; then she stepped away and he knew he'd lost.

"Please don't rush me on this, Kirk," she begged, and hope rose again within him. It wasn't total defeat, merely a postponement of victory. He studied her for several moments, hoping to discern what was inside her that made her hesitate, but it was as if she had pulled a shield down over her soul. Finally, he nodded. "I'll wait, sweetheart. For as long as you need me to. Just don't stop loving me."

"That," she said, "I can promise." They exchanged a hard and desperate kiss, then Liss looked up at him. "I want you, Kirk. I want to make love with you tonight."

"I know," he said. "I want that, too, but . . . No, Liss. If I can wait for your answer, then I can wait for that. I love you, sweetheart. Good night."

She lay very still in her bed, listening to the house settling, to the wind rising to blow the clouds east over the mountains, to her own heart beating. Feeling it beat faster, she slipped out of bed and put on a gossamer robe over her sheer nightgown. Mouth dry and palms wet, she quietly opened her door and stepped into the darkened corridor.

No one person, she told herself, had the right to make all the decisions that affected two. And besides, maybe this would help allay her doubts. . . .

Silently she opened Kirk's door and slipped inside. She closed it behind her without a sound, but he turned from the window, a dark figure outlined against moonlight that created a halo of gold in his dark blond hair and glistened on his bare shoulders.

Without speaking, she went to him, sliding one arm around his middle and resting her head on him. She touched his chest with her fingertips, stroking through the curly hair there, and felt him tremble. His arms closed around her convulsively, crushing her to him, straining her closer as he drew in a long, harsh breath. "Ah, Liss," he murmured, running his hand over her hair. "Why, love?"

She tilted her head back, wishing she could see him, but he was still nothing more than a dark shape with the moonlight slanting in over his shoulder. "Because I am sure about this," she said. "I wish I could be as sure about the rest of it, but I know I need you, Kirk. I love you, and I'll leave if you ask me to. I'm praying you won't."

He cupped her face in his hands. "I could no more ask that of you than ask you to give up your children for me. That's all I was concerned with."

"Don't be." She ran her hands over his shoulders, marveling at how smooth his skin was in contrast to the hardness of his muscles. "My in-laws can't see behind closed doors. And you-know-who can't hear with her hearing aids out."

He tangled his hand in her hair and turned her so the moonlight bathed her face. She stood on tiptoe, placed her lips against his throat, and kissed him. Kirk shuddered at the softness of her lips against him, the silken touch of her night-clothes on his body. "I want you naked," he said.

She touched his face with a gentle hand, loving him so much, she hurt inside from the force of it. "I want to be naked."

He turned his head quickly and kissed her fingers. "You taste good. Do you taste that good all over? I'm going to—" He didn't finish, but groaned softly as he shoved her robe off her shoulders. He undid the three small buttons at the top of her nightgown and slid it over her breasts. It glided down her arms, her belly, her hips, falling to the floor so slowly, the fabric was a sensuous caress that elicited a sharp gasp from her. Turning her fully to the moonlight, he looked at her, his gaze sweeping over her, his fingers touching everywhere—outlining a cheekbone, teasing a nipple into rigidity, stroking over skin, touching hair, making stomach muscles flutter wildly. Her legs could scarcely support her by the time he lifted her into his arms and carried her to his bed. "Ah, Liss, Liss, I need you now!"

"Yes," she breathed, and accepted the weight of him on her, loved it, met it with a savage need of her own. Her nails raked his back gently, down over his waist and hips, then her palms shaped themselves to his buttocks as she strained to get nearer to him. "Hurry," she pleaded. "Kirk, hurry . . ."

But he continued to excite her, tease her, evoking responses he'd known would be there, responses he sensed surprised her, even embarrassed her at times, especially when he switched on his reading light to see her better. She turned to hide her face from him.

"Open your eyes, sweetheart. Look at me. Show me what you feel."

"I've never felt anything like this," she said, keeping her face turned away. When he refrained from touching her until she complied, though, she opened her eyes. He exulted at their incandescent glow and smiled at their yearning shyness.

"I have never seen anyone as beautiful as you," he whispered, continuing his gentle exploration of her body, worshiping her with his hands, his gaze, his mouth.

"Oh, please," she cried softly. "I can't take any more, Kirk."

"Ah, you ask so sweetly," he said, and moved

over her as she writhed beneath him in wanton, voluptuous pleasure. He took her mouth even as she swung her legs around him, laced her hands over his back, and pulled him to her, joining their bodies at last in a wild and desperate surge of passion.

Completion came almost at once in a thundering rush of blood and a quivering arching of muscle and spine, as two bodies blended in the ancient harmony of love. When it had spent itself, Kirk lay on his side, Liss cradled half on top of him, and he stroked his hand up and down the length of her torso. Slowly, their breathing became less labored, their heartbeats returned to normal, and they smiled into each other's eyes. They kissed softly, nuzzled and cuddled, enjoying each other in the shining afterglow of their love.

When she felt she could lift a hand, Liss outlined his eyebrows with one finger and laughed softly.

He kissed the tip of her nose. "What's funny?"

"I feel as if we've just invented sex."

He grinned and stretched. "Didn't we?"

She nodded, looking up at him and shading her eyes against the glare of his bedside lamp. "I think so. We made a miracle."

He shut the light off and made a mental note to put in a smaller bulb, a softer, more romantic one. He thought that from here on in, he'd be doing a lot less reading after he went to bed. "You're the miracle," he said. "Don't go away, Liss. Oh, Lord, don't ever go away!"

He pulled her close to him under the covers, then leaned up over her and looked at her fine profile outlined by moonlight. "I forgot to do it," he said, tracing the curves of her cheekbone and chin. "After all that wondering, all that dreaming and anticipating, when it happened, I was too busy to look."

"Look at what?"

"At what happens to your eyes when you climax."

He saw her teeth gleam as she smiled. "I think I go blind."

"No kidding?" He slowly drew his hand from her neck all the way down to her hip. "Shall we find out?"

Liss's sigh was tremulous. "Why not?" she whispered. "We have so many things to find out about each other. . . ."

Ten

Two days before Christmas, in a flurry of snow and bags and laughter, Kirk's mother arrived. She hugged him exuberantly, shed her outdoor clothing, heaping it into his arms, then turned to assess Liss. She was smiling, and her gray eyes, so like Kirk's, were sharp and searching.

"How do you do?" Liss said, suddenly shy and afraid of what those searching eyes would see. She fought down a big dose of irrational panic, telling herself that Kirk's mother could not tell simply by looking at her what she and Kirk did together while the household slept. After showing the older woman to her room and helping Kirk carry up the multitude of bags, she forced herself to make Betty, as Kirk's mother insisted she be called, comfortable and at home in the living room. Then she tried to escape, murmuring something about dinner and Kirk wanting time alone with his mother.

"Hey, relax," he said, laughing as he jumped to his feet and pinned her to his side. "You don't need to run away."

"I'm not, but—"

"Come on, sweetheart. Don't look so scared. Mom likes you, don't you, Mom?"

"Of course I do." Betty winked at Liss, then lifted her son's arm from around the younger woman and said sternly, "Behave. You're embarrassing the girl." She shoved him across the hall toward the kitchen. "Go play with your horse or something, and give us a chance to get to know each other."

Liss cast an appealing glance at Kirk, who shrugged, grinned, and sauntered out.

When they were alone, Betty said, "I'm really delighted to meet you, you know. Any girl who can make my son beam the way you do has to be important to him. I never thought I'd see the day he'd succumb," she added with a laugh. "I bet there are a dozen women in two provinces who'd kill to know how you did it." She leaned forward conspiratorially. "What is your secret?"

"I . . . uh . . ."

"Oh, rats, now *I'm* embarrassing you," Betty said, shaking her head. "I'm sorry. I tend to speak and then think. It's a pretty new love affair, isn't it?" While Liss sought words with which to reply, Betty let her off the hook. "How about showing me around? Ambrose bought this place long after I was out of the picture, and I must confess to a certain amount of curiosity about what he provided for my successor. I understand he was married to your aunt?" She looked wistful for a moment. "I hope he was happy with her, though it was for a very short time, wasn't it?"

Liss nodded, beginning to relax, and led the way into the playroom. "A little over a year. I was a young child at the time, so I don't remember either of them. Ambrose kept no contact with my family after Aunt Cynthia died. I don't think he liked my dad very much."

Betty smiled as she turned in a circle, admiring the comfortable room, the decorated tree, the child-made garlands. "Ambrose didn't like many people," she said. "He found it difficult to trust. I loved him, you know, and I felt very sorry for the things he missed in life." She sat on the sofa and looked up at Liss. "That's why I sent him my son. I think sons are important to men, maybe more than they are to us, though I love Kirk as much as I'm sure you love your sons." She looked wistful again. "I never got over wanting a daughter. How about you? Wouldn't a little girl-child be a total delight?"

Betty Allbright was a total delight, Liss decided. Before the afternoon was over, she had captivated Ryan and Jason by teaching them how to navigate on the tiny bear-paw snowshoes she'd brought as "pre-Christmas" presents. The next day, while the boys napped, she sent Kirk and Liss "outside to play" and baked gingerbread men for the tree, enlisting Mrs. Healey's "experienced" hand at decorating them.

Liss stared in disbelief as Betty and Mrs. Healey hung the cookies from the tree, laughing and chatting like old friends, then nearly fainted when Mrs. Healey brushed Jason's hair out of his eyes and asked if he was excited about hanging his stocking that night.

It was, Liss thought, feeling limp and exhausted after it was all over, the most wonderful Christmas she'd ever experienced. She remembered especially the moment she opened her gift from Mrs. Healey and found a pair of bright pink knitted slippers with a small, handwritten note pinned to them. Her jaw had dropped, she knew, as her eyes instinctively sought Kirk's. He sat stunned at her side, staring down at his enormous purple slippers, with drawstrings and tassels. Silently they exchanged notes, which were duplicates, word for word: *For those cold trips across the hall at night.*

They collapsed in laughter together, but refused to share the joke, though Betty threatened them with no turkey dinner. Finally, wiping tears of mirth from her eyes, Liss managed to look at Mrs. Healey.

The old lady sat staring coldly at her; then, so quickly it might never have been, she winked.

"I do love Christmas!" Liss whispered to Kirk.

He smiled. "And I do love you!" He lifted his coffee mug and touched hers. "Merry Christmas, sweetheart. The first of many we'll share."

"What are you doing in here all alone?" Kirk asked the afternoon of the twenty-seventh as he entered the playroom. Liss sat curled on the couch, not reading, merely staring into the fire. Brooding, he thought as he shut the door. "Are you okay?"

"Sure," she said. "I'm fine."

"You don't look fine. You got the blues because the boys' grandparents are coming tonight?"

She smiled faintly. "I guess so. Two weeks is a long time. I don't want the kids to go, but I have no valid reason to stop them. Besides, they want to go. I'm being selfish. It's only because I'll miss them so much."

He sat beside her and picked her up, cuddling her on his lap and nuzzling his face into the curve of her neck. "What if I promise you won't have time to miss them?"

She smiled, her blues beginning to ease. "What do you have in mind?"

Without words, he showed her, kissing her until she was dizzy. She leaned back against the arm of the sofa, gazing up at him, her eyes warm with the luminous glow he loved to see.

"Kids asleep?" he asked, his breath ragged. She nodded, running a finger around his left ear. "And Mom and Mrs. H. won't be back till four-thirty?" She nodded again, then put a hand behind his head and pulled him down to her. His desire escalated with such rapidity, Kirk was out of control before he knew it.

With a swift, economical motion, he stripped off her sweater, then his own. He undid her bra and bent to kiss her nipples, to draw them into his mouth.

"Oh, Lord, how I want you!" he moaned. "I've understood your reluctance to come to me while my mother's here, Liss, but she's not here now. We're alone. Love me, baby. Love me now. . . ."

Liss spread her palms over his chest, feeling the heavy pounding of his heart. It had been too long for her too. "Yes," she whispered. "Oh, yes." And she stretched out on the sofa, welcoming his weight as he lay half on top of her. He caressed her breasts and kissed her mouth, lifting his head only to whisper in her ear how much he had missed her and what he planned to do about it.

They never heard the knocking, never heard the door open, never knew they weren't alone until an angry gasp sliced through the air and a shrill voice demanded, "And where might my innocent little grandsons be while you're carrying on like this in broad daylight?"

It was Kirk who moved, sitting up and shielding Liss with his body. He glared at a shocked Kristy, who was frantically pulling on a rotund, bald man and a short, stocky woman while apologizing profusely, confusedly, saying she didn't know, she should never have barged in. But she simply didn't know and she was so sorry, but these folks were looking for Liss and had got lost, so'd she led the way to the ranch and then brought them inside when nobody answered the door, and she knew the boys were normally in the playroom and . . .

"Kristy, shut the door," Kirk said. Not until she had complied did he turn back to Liss and hand her her bra and sweater.

"Lord, sweetheart," he said, shocked by her pale face. "I'm sorry! I did it again, didn't I? When am I going to learn not to touch you unless we're locked away somewhere and—"

"Kirk. Stop. It's all right. Truly it is." Liss fully believed that . . . until she faced her in-laws.

"Mr. and Mrs. McCall," she said, trying to keep her voice from shaking as hard as her body shook, "I'd like to present Kirk Allbright, co-owner of Whittier Ranch and . . ." Panic set in, making it impossible for her to meet those two sets of accusing eyes, face that pair of tight, pursed mouths and the disapproval, the silent, awful rebuke, without some kind of explanation, some kind of reinforcement. She clutched Kirk's hand where it rested on her shoulder and added in a rush, "My—my husband-to-be."

Kirk's hand slowly fell from her shoulder as he reached out to accept the hand Mr. McCall offered him.

"Well," Mrs. McCall said with a sniff. "You're certainly nothing like my son. I'm surprised to hear that Phyllis means to marry you."

"So am I," Kirk murmured blandly. Liss was the

only one who knew that the freckles on his cheeks didn't normally show so starkly.

"The boys are still napping," she told the McCalls. "We weren't expecting you until later."

"That," said her father-in-law, "was quite obvious. Wake the children, please, Phyllis. We want to leave at once. There's a storm front moving in." It was no request.

Liss glanced at Kirk and knew there was a storm front moving in from that direction, too, but there was nothing she could do to stop it. As soon as the boys were happily busy showing off their loot to their adoring grandparents, Kirk grabbed Liss by the arm and all but dragged her out to his workshop in the barn.

"Now," he said, shoving her down onto the bench and looming over her, his fists on his hips. "We are going to have a very serious talk, Ms. Tremayne!"

"You're mad."

"You're damned right I'm mad! And hurt. And mortified and humiliated and ashamed and a lot of other words I could think of, but damn good and mad just about covers it perfectly! First, you refuse to marry me because you need time to think about it; then, the minute your in-laws catch us doing something that their dirty little minds might consider immoral, I'm suddenly your beloved fiancé and that makes it all right for us to be stripping each other naked in broad daylight. Forget it, Liss. I have more pride than that. If I were going to marry you, I'd want a hell of a lot better reason than your fear of the McCalls!"

She shot to her feet. No way was she going to sit like a recalcitrant child while this monster of a man towered over her and bellowed at her. "*If you* were going to marry me? Meaning you're not? You don't want to be known as my husband-to-be?"

"No, dammit, not under those circumstances!" he yelled. "Liss, can't you see—"

"I see one thing only," she shouted back at him. "You don't want to marry me. You never did, if something like this can change your mind so fast! I don't know why I ever believed you in the first place, when all my instincts told me it couldn't be true. Why do you think I never said yes? Because I sensed deep inside that you were only using me, that I was a convenience to you. What's changed, Kirk? Have you got someone else to look after the house and . . . the other things? Someone more experienced, maybe, a better lover? Someone . . . taller? Someone with bigger boobs?"

"What the hell are you talking about?" he roared, ramming a hand through his hair.

"You know damned well what I'm talking about! If this is what you want to use as an excuse to go after Gina again, fine. Go ahead and use it."

For the second time in an hour, she watched his freckles pop out across his cheekbones. He grabbed her by the upper arms and shook her. "I don't want to marry Gina," he said raggedly. "I've never wanted to marry her!"

"And you never wanted to marry me either, or anyone else. You proposed to me out of sheer expediency, because you felt you couldn't make me stay otherwise, not once you knew my photography was starting to pay off. Do you think I didn't notice that you asked me to marry you the very day I got my first check? The thought of my independence scared you, didn't it, Kirk?"

He didn't deny it. He only stared at her, and she went on, her rage creating a fine haze before her eyes. All the hurts, all the losses, all the pain of the past seemed encompassed in this one moment of his rejection. "It must have come as a shock when I didn't leap at the chance to put an end to your bachelorhood. But one thing you'll have to realize, Kirk. This city girl isn't quite as stupid as you thought. I can look after myself and my children, and if you don't need me, I don't need you!"

He glared at her silently, then spun around and strode out of the barn, leaving her shaking and sick and icy cold as she listened to his truck drive away.

With her chin tilted high, she strode from the barn, not looking back. Less than an hour later, she sat in the back seat of the McCalls' car with her children on either side of her. She held them tightly, telling herself that this was the right thing to do. She didn't love Kirk. She didn't want him. She hated the ranch and all it stood for and was glad to be leaving.

But if that was the case, why was she crying all those silent tears?

"Why, Ms. Tremayne!" Lester Brown stood to welcome Liss into his drab office and seated her in a hard chair. "Happy New Year. I hope you enjoyed your first Christmas at Whittier Ranch. I was surprised to hear you were back in the city. Just here for a little visit, I suppose. How are the children settling in?"

"They're visiting their grandparents while I look for a place to live," Liss said. She bowed her head and stared at her linked hands for a moment, then glanced back up. "I've left the ranch. I'm sorry I couldn't live up to what my uncle wanted of me, but I've begun selling photographs recently, so I'll be able to pay back the money you advanced me. It may take time, but I'll do it."

Lester tented his neatly manicured fingers and gazed at her over them. "My dear, I'm sorry things didn't work out for you up there, but there's no need for you to pay anything back. Your uncle knew you might not be happy at the ranch and made provisions that will enable you to live elsewhere if you want. I wasn't permitted to tell you until you'd given ranch life a good try, but now I can. You're to have one hundred thousand dollars, paid at once, which will cancel your claim on the ranch."

A hundred thousand dollars? Her head spun. Where was Kirk going to get that kind of money? How many cows would he have to sell? Appalled, she stared at Lester. "No!" she said. "I can't take that."

"But you must, my dear. It's in the will."

"I don't care. Tell him he can keep it, tell him I died and left it to him, tell him anything you want, but I'm not taking that money from Kirk! Do you have any idea what that kind of a loss would mean to Kir—to the ranch? He'd have to sell stock, and without cows, there won't be calves. Without calves, there won't be steers. Without steers, there'll be no beef, and no money to buy new stock! No, Mr. Brown. The ranch couldn't handle that kind of loss."

Lester looked at her compassionately. "You came to care about . . . um, the ranch, then?"

"Yes. Of course. It's a wonderful place. I learned to love . . . it. Please, don't take that money from him, Mr. Brown. It would be disastrous! Why, Kirk nearly killed himself during every storm, because he couldn't afford to lose even one cow. I'm sorry. I know Uncle Ambrose meant well, but I can't accept it. I won't."

Swiftly she got to her feet. "Excuse me. I must go. But as I said, I mean to repay every cent of what you advanced me. It's not my money. It's Kirk's, and he needs all of it."

"My dear, please," Lester said, standing quickly. "Wait, won't you? Let me explain. Let me—"

She shook her head, fighting tears. "I won't take money that Kirk needs to run the ranch. Don't you know how important it is to him, Mr. Brown? How much he loves it? It's his life. It was going to be mine, too, and my children's, but I was stupid and weak and scared and let it matter too much that he loved me as much for my cake as he did for myself and . . . and . . . I'm sorry, Mr. Brown. Goodbye."

"The money doesn't come from the ranch," Lester said, but Liss didn't hear. She'd opened the door and run into a wall.

She looked up, way up. Her tears blurred Kirk's face, and the sight of him only made her cry harder. "He wants you to give me a whole pile of money. I won't take it, Kirk. I'll come back to the ranch and be loved for my chocolate cake and sex before I'll let you ruin the ranch that way."

"Chocolate cake?" he asked, tilting his hat to the back of his head. "Sex?" He bent down and quickly kissed her. "Never mind. Don't answer. Just come home with me, Liss. I need you, love. Please come home."

Liss shook from the force of her weeping. She couldn't even question why he was there, although she suspected Lester Brown had something to do with it. All that mattered was that Kirk was there. And he was holding her, stroking her hair, looking down at her, his eyes full of questions and love and sadness and need.

"Cakes and kisses," she said, hiccuping. "Supper and sex. What Mrs. Healey said you and Ambrose wanted from your housekeepers. Gina can't cook, she'd make a terrible rancher's wife, so you asked me instead and . . . Isn't your mother going to stay and take over the kitchen?"

"My mother and Mrs. Healey are going on a Caribbean cruise together."

She blinked in surprise, then said, "You see? You need my cakes."

Her mouth trembled. Her chin quivered. He planted a finger on it, square over her scar. "I need your kisses," he said.

"Why?"

"Because I love you." When she continued to look at him with a thousand doubts in her exotic eyes, he lost his patience—exactly what he'd told Lester he wouldn't do. "For the love of Mike, woman!" he bellowed. "What does it take to convince you?"

"Is that why—really why—you want to marry me?"

He drew in a deep breath. "Yes, Liss. That's really why. It's the only reason why. If you want to spend all your time taking pictures, I'll hire a damned cook, but it's you I want in my home, in my bed, in my heart, because I love you, city girl."

She smiled, then reached way, way up and kissed him. "Maybe you'll have to stop calling me that," she murmured, her whole body seeming to glow with her love for him.

He looked down at her three-inch heels and shook his head. "Nope. I love you just the way you are, city shoes and all. Keep wearing those and I won't get such a crick in my neck."

She flung her arms around his neck and laughed. "But would it be all right if I kicked them off now and then and got hay down my back?"

"Come on home," he said, "and we'll see."

THE EDITOR'S CORNER

With the six marvelous **LOVESWEPT**s coming your way next month, it certainly will be the season to be jolly. Reading the best romances from the finest authors—what better way to enter into the holiday spirit?

Leading our fabulous lineup is the ever-popular Fayrene Preston with **SATAN'S ANGEL**, LOVESWEPT #510. Nicholas Santini awakes after a car crash and thinks he's died and gone to heaven—why else would a beautiful angel be at his side? But Angel Smith is a flesh-and-blood woman who makes him burn with a desire that lets him know he's very much alive. Angel's determined to work a miracle on this magnificent man, to drive away the pain—and the peril—that torments him. A truly wonderful story, written with sizzling sensuality and poignant emotions—one of Fayrene's best!

How appropriate that Gail Douglas's newest LOVESWEPT is titled **AFTER HOURS**, #511, for that's when things heat up between Casey McIntyre and Alex McLean. Alex puts his business—and heart—on the line when he works *very* closely with Casey to save his newspaper. He's been betrayed before, but Casey inspires trust . . . and brings him to a fever pitch of sensual excitement. She never takes orders from anyone, yet she can't seem to deny Alex's passionate demands. A terrific book, from start to finish.

Sandra Chastain weaves her magical touch in **THE-JUDGE AND THE GYPSY**, LOVESWEPT #512. When Judge Rasch Webber unknowingly shatters her father's dream, Savannah Ramey vows a Gypsy's revenge: She would tantalize him beyond reason, awakening longings he's denied, then steal what he most loves. She couldn't know she'd be entangled in a web of desire, drawn to the velvet caress of Rasch's voice and the ecstatic fulfillment in his arms. You'll be thoroughly enchanted with this story of forbidden love.

The combination of love and laughter makes **MIDNIGHT KISS** by Marcia Evanick, LOVESWEPT #513, completely irresistible. To Autumn O'Neil, Thane Clayborne is a sexy stick-in-the-mud, and she delights in making him lose control. True, running a little wild is not Thane's style, but Autumn's seductive beauty tempts him to let go. Still, she's afraid that the man who bravely sacrificed a dream for another's happiness could never care for a woman who ran scared when it counted most. Another winner from Marcia Evanick!

With his tight jeans, biker boots, and heartbreak-blue eyes, Michael Hayward is a **TEMPTATION FROM THE PAST**, LOVESWEPT #514, by Cindy Gerard. January Stewart has never seen a sexier man, but she knows he's more trouble that she can handle. Intrigued by the dedicated lawyer, Michael wants to thaw January's cool demeanor and light her fire. Is he the one who would break down her defenses and cast away her secret pain? Your heart will be stirred by this touching story.

A fitting final course is **JUST DESSERTS** by Theresa Gladden, LOVESWEPT #515. Caitlin MacKenzie has had it with being teased by her new housemate, Drew Daniels, and she retaliates with a cream pie in his face! Pleased that serious Caitie has a sense of humor to match her lovely self, Drew begins an ardent pursuit. She would fit so perfectly in the future he's mapped out, but Catie has dreams of her own, dreams that could cost her what she has grown to treasure. A sweet and sexy romance—what more could anybody want?

FANFARE presents four truly spectacular books this month! Don't miss bestselling Amanda Quick's **RENDEZ-VOUS**. From London's most exclusive club to an imposing country manor, comes this provocative tale about a free-thinking beauty, a reckless charmer, and a love that defied all logic. **MIRACLE**, by beloved LOVESWEPT author Deborah Smith, is the unforgettable contemporary romance of passion and the collision of worlds, where a man and a woman who couldn't have been more different learn that love may be improbable, but never impossible.

Immensely talented Rosalind Laker delivers the exquisite historical **CIRCLE OF PEARLS.** In England during the days of plague and fire, Julia Pallister's greatest test comes from an unexpected quarter—the man she calls enemy, a man who will stop at nothing to win her heart. And in **FOREVER,** by critically acclaimed Theresa Weir, we witness the true power of love. Sammy Thoreau had been pronounced a lost cause, but from the moment Dr. Rachel Collins lays eyes on him, she knows she would do anything to help the bad-boy journalist learn to live again.

Happy reading!

With every good wish for a holiday filled with the best things in life,

Nita Taublib

Nita Taublib
Associate Publisher/LOVESWEPT
Publishing Associate/FANFARE